BJD

SPECIAL MESSAGE TO READERS

This book is published under the auspices of

THE ULVERSCROFT FOUNDATION

(registered charity No. 264873 UK)

Established in 1972 to provide funds for research, diagnosis and treatment of eye diseases. Examples of contributions made are: —

A Children's Assessment Unit at Moorfield's Hospital, London.

•

Twin operating theatres at the Western Ophthalmic Hospital, London.

•

A Chair of Ophthalmology at the Royal Australian College of Ophthalmologists.

•

The Ulverscroft Children's Eye Unit at the Great Ormond Street Hospital For Sick Children, London.

You can help further the work of the Foundation by making a donation or leaving a legacy. Every contribution, no matter how small, is received with gratitude. Please write for details to:

THE ULVERSCROFT FOUNDATION,
The Green, Bradgate Road, Anstey,
Leicester LE7 7FU, England.
Telephone: (0116) 236 4325

In Australia write to:

THE ULVERSCROFT FOUNDATION,
c/o The Royal Australian and New Zealand
College of Ophthalmologists,
94-98 Chalmers Street, Surry Hills,
N.S.W. 2010, Australia

RAW DEAL AT PASCO SPRINGS

When ex-lawman Tom Mallory won the Diamond T ranch in a poker game, he thought Lady Luck had truly smiled on him. This impression swiftly changed when he rode straight into a bushwhacking. So began a curious chain of events that led him to resume his former profession. It soon became clear that someone had designs on the Diamond T ranch and would stop at nothing to get it. Murder was afoot and, as tempers frayed, Tom realized that he had to find out who was behind it all . . .

CLAY MORE

RAW DEAL AT PASCO SPRINGS

Complete and Unabridged

LINFORD
Leicester

First published in Great Britain in 2004 by
Robert Hale Limited
London

First Linford Edition
published 2005
by arrangement with
Robert Hale Limited
London

British Library CIP Data

More, Clay
Raw deal at Pasco Springs.—Large print ed.—
Linford western library
1. Western stories
2. Large type books
I. Title
823.9′2 [F]

ISBN 1–84395–775–2

Published by
F. A. Thorpe (Publishing)
Anstey, Leicestershire

Set by Words & Graphics Ltd.
Anstey, Leicestershire
Printed and bound in Great Britain by
T. J. International Ltd., Padstow, Cornwall

This book is printed on acid-free paper

For Big Jake — who loved the
Old West

Prologue

Bathed in perspiration Jake Trent woke from his dream with a fitful start, only to realize that the noise of the mob was no illusion, no figment of his unconscious mind. Shouts, jeers, whiskey-fired oaths of indignation, retribution and malignant intent seemed to gather in intensity with each passing moment, alerting him to the advancing menace.

He jumped to his feet, hands clenching the steel bars of the cell.

Burnett, the recently deputized bar-dog was peering through the window slats into the night. At the sight of the flaring torches carried in the front of the advancing mob he visibly trembled. His scrawny Adam's apple rose and descended in slow motion, as if every drop of spit in his head had evaporated through sheer fear. 'The hell with this!' He looked at his prisoner and shook his head. 'And the hell with you!' he cried, tossing the keys of the cell on the desk as he dashed for the back door.

Trent felt his heart race fit to burst out of his chest. Then before he knew it the mob came like a wave, hurtling against the door of the sheriff's office. Axes, hammers, boots and shoulders made short work of the door, then in they flooded, a sea of half-crazed humanity. He tried to retreat into a corner of the cell, knowing only too well that it was useless to do so. There was nowhere to go, no one to help.

Someone had found the keys and the cell door was quickly unlocked and wrenched open, then they were upon him. Like the cornered animal that he was he struck right and left, desperate to go down with a fight, because there was no point in pleading for clemency, for a fair trial, for justice.

Battered and bruised, his red hair matted with blood and one eye half-closed, his hands were bound behind him and he was manhandled outside and forced along the main street.

'Rapist! Murdering dog! String him up!' The cries and taunts were like whips on raw flesh.

They formed a ring of torches round the old cottonwood outside the town. A rope was deftly flung over a convenient branch, then he was physically lifted onto the back of a pony.

His mind scarcely able to comprehend what was happening, he scanned the mob, recognizing men he had worked with, enjoyed a drink with, even entertained at his ranch. People he had once considered friends. But now their faces were anything but friendly. Fired up with whiskey and a bloodlust, they wanted his death. Together with the fear he felt a profound sadness. He was never going to see his new wife again, nor his boy.

'Stretch the bastard's neck!' cried out one drunken pock-marked youth who had worked for him the year before, until he had fired him for mistreating a pony.

At the back of the mob the more respectable folk stood and watched. The town elders, the clever ones who ran things and had no need to toil themselves. And among them he saw one face that bore no expression of hate, anger or lust. There was written across the countenance nothing except unmistakable triumph. In that instant he realized the man who was responsible for all this. The man who had framed him and brought him — an innocent man — to the brink of death, the guest of honour at a necktie party.

'Go to hell, you redheaded bastard,' someone shouted, slapping the pony's rump, causing it to lurch forward.

The rope tightened about his neck, and then the pony disappeared from under him. His fear was replaced by a tide of anger and hatred, which consumed him — until the moment his neck broke and he was released from his mortal coil.

1

The sun was riding high in a cloudless sky by the time Tom Mallory reached the end of the trail that zigzagged down from the mesa.

'Looks like you win the bet,' he said good-humouredly to the hammer-headed roan, as he spied the stream that bubbled down from a hidden spring in the rocks. 'I guess that redheaded punter was telling the truth after all. And that means that Lady Luck truly has dropped a ranch in our hands.'

The roan whinnied again, his nostrils flaring as if to repeat an injunction that he'd smelled water for the past half-hour.

Mallory laughed as they reached the stream. He dismounted and let the animal lap up water. 'You've earned it my friend,' he said as he replenished his canteen, then drank himself. After the three-day journey across the undulating south-western desert with its dry gulches, outcrops of parched rock interspersed with clumps of mesquite and saguaro cacti it tasted sweeter than any drink he had ever partaken of.

He looked at his reflection in the stream, grinned at the accumulation of dust on his all-black duds. He slid his fingers through his thick black hair and shook free a patina of fine sand. He resolved that one of his first stops in Pasco Springs was going to be the nearest bathhouse.

Leading the reluctant roan across the stream to savour some of the short grass that grew on the banks, he struck a light to a cheroot. 'It's either tobacco or grass for me too,' he mused sorrowfully, feeling slightly light-headed as the tobacco, the blazing heat and water on an empty stomach combined together, making him realize how hungry he was, and how angry with himself that he'd missed a shot at that lone jack rabbit the day before.

He shrugged the thought aside as he savoured the cigar together with the realization that the town of Pasco Springs could only be a few miles away now. Images of food, a cold beer and a bed came comfortingly to his mind.

His eye spied a handful of fat blowflies hovering around the roan's rump, prompting him to let the reins trail while he fanned his hat to disperse them. 'Let's have a look-see at that bullet wound of yours,' he said as he tenderly stroked the hide around the inflamed graze, which he had packed with mud and fly larvae he'd plucked from the maggoty carcass of a desert spadefoot. 'Appears that you win another bet,' he joked to the roan. 'Some of your livestock has growed up and learned to fly. Might as well spare some of 'Adam's wine' on the critters that still has growing room.'

He poured a little water from his canteen to moisten the sun-baked mud and the wriggling silkwhite bodies of the maggots. 'We don't want these to dry up and die when they've done such a fine job keeping your wound clean.'

With a look back up the way he had come, just as he had been doing automatically every so often over the past three days, he remounted and nudged the roan on up the trail.

Chewing on the cheroot he grinned as his hand brushed the polished butt of the Spencer rifle protruding from the scabbard on the side of the Texas rig. The gun was a near antique, the spoils of some half-remembered poker game, as indeed were the saddle itself and most of his belongings, yet with its well-oiled action and cannon-like .52 cartridges it had proved to be a powerful dissuader. And in the unpredictable line of work that he as a professional gambler enjoyed, there were times when such a tool was a welcome friend — especially if he had to leave a town in a hurry.

'Wonder if the cuss was aiming for real or not,' he mused to the back of the roan's head. 'I don't think it was a serious bushwhack attempt, more an expression of disdain. And if that's so, then to just graze your rump means that the shootist was some deadly shot — whoever he was.'

With the practised memory of a good poker player he ran over the faces of the players in that last game he'd played in Hacksville. Could have been any of five or six that he'd relieved of their bundles. But one had lost a damned sight more than a bundle of cash.

The ready smile of the young red-haired man flashed in front of his mind's eye. A good-looking youngster by the name of Jeff Trent. A likeable sort of guy, Mallory reckoned, as long as he stayed away from whiskey. And of course that was exactly what the kid had not done. Mallory had scooped the pot, including the deed to one Diamond T ranch, duly signed over and witnessed.

'Yep, could have been him,' Mallory said aloud. 'And that being the case I'm betting it was a well-aimed miss. Just an angry parting shot from a hot-headed loser recovering from a helluva hang-over.'

His mind played over the event of his leaving town the next morning before sun-up, generally a good time to bid a town farewell.

A single shot rang out and the roan bucked once, then made to tear into a gallop. Mallory gripped hard with his knees and dropping the reins let the beast have its head. He spun round in the saddle with the Spencer already at his shoulder, and let off a couple of shots in the direction of his assailant. Whether he scored a hit or not, though the chances were only slight, the shots had seemed to dissuade any further reaction or pursuit. He rode fast for a mile or so before he stopped to examine and treat the wound on the roan's rump.

'But it was a fair game,' he said, almost as if to reassure the roan of his integrity. 'All growed-up men with growed-up decisions and notions of how to play draw poker.'

The horse nickered and Mallory leaned forward to give its neck a good pat. He had become truly fond of the beast, which he had won off a drover in Tucson, and that surprised him. Ever since the day Annabelle had been killed he had expunged any sort of sentiment from his being. No ties, no commitments. Live by his wits, by his skills, that was his way. He had decided to live each day and see what cards Lady Luck dealt him.

He looked at the changeable land ahead. Purple spired and pinnacled peaks stretched across the northern horizon, while immediately ahead of him were wooded gullies and outcrops of red rock. Beyond that, a welcome sight after the sagebrush semi-desert he had traversed, lay savannahs of grass with occasional thin ribbon streams that gleamed silver in the sunlight.

'Yessir, looks like Lady Luck has smiled on me and you, old hoss. Somewhere over there is a ranch with a ranch house and veranda waiting for me to sit and sip cool lemonade on.'

As if understanding the gambler's monologue, the roan whinnied.

Mallory laughed. 'OK. And maybe we'll find a corral with some young filly just pining her heart out for a good-looking critter like you.'

* * *

It was mid-afternoon when he reached the rim of a wide gully, the sloping sides of which were covered with a startling range of vegetation — spruce, juniper, paloverde and cactus.

He was picking his way down through the trees when what seemed like a whole fusillade of gunfire erupted ahead of him. It was followed by a series of diminishing echoes from around the gully walls, which made him realize there were fewer guns than he had at first imagined. In a trice he had the Spencer out of its scabbard as he scanned the area to see the source of the shooting.

A balloon of smoke halfway up the far incline showed from whence one of the shots had come, while the crack of a handgun on the gully floor indicated another.

Realizing that he was not the target of either gun he urged the roan onwards, heading for an outcrop of huge boulders that would afford him cover. As he momentarily left the screen of trees he caught his first sight of one of the participants. A man was lying on the ground, struggling to drag his leg out from under his dead mount. One arm hung useless and the sleeve of his shirt appeared to be soaked in blood.

Another shot and a telltale puff of smoke from the trees drew the wounded man's attention and he fired three shots in that direction. Mallory could see that they were futile, since he was woefully out of range with a handgun. Apart from that, it looked as if he was shooting awkwardly, as if with his unaccustomed hand.

Then the unexpected made Mallory

rein the roan in. A hooded man in a long duster coat suddenly appeared from trees fifty yards to the left of the first rifleman. A Winchester barked angrily and the man under the horse cried out as he was slammed back on the ground. He lay ominously still, the gun falling from his fist.

'Murdering bushwhackers!' growled Mallory, raising his Spencer and letting off a shot at the hooded figure in the duster coat.

Immediately, two guns were trained on him and he felt a gush of air against one cheek as a bullet whistled past, while a second gouged out a chunk from his saddle horn. The roan reared and Mallory instinctively knew that now was no time for bronc busting. He had dallied too long in the open and would never reach the shelter of the boulder without catching a bullet. He let go with his knees, allowed his feet to slip out of the stirrups and let himself be tossed backwards into a patch of greasewood.

He landed amid a hail of bullets that tore into the patch. Ignoring the winding he had received, functioning on pure survival instinct he slid sidewinder fashion further into the heart of the brush. Peering through the tangle of greasewood he saw that the duster coat had vanished back into the trees.

A bullet zinged into the brush close to the spot where Mallory had landed and he returned fire the moment he saw the telltale balloon of smoke from the trees. Expecting a counter-shot he immediately rolled to his left and drew one of his brace of Navy Colts in readiness.

As if on cue a bullet tore itself into the bushes where he had been, gouging out a mess of dirt. He saw another puff of smoke emerge from the same thicket of trees, then he rolled back, firing the Navy Colt as he passed the spot he had originally been in. He kept on rolling.

Two shots rang out, each zoning in on the spot he had fired from, covering him with dirt.

Coming to rest he saw two dispersing balloons of gunsmoke fifty feet apart.

Clever bastards! They were trying to triangulate him, just like they had done with the guy down on the gully floor, whoever he was. Used as he was to dealing with potential sandbaggings, Mallory realized the seriousness of his position. These murderous *hombres* were prepared to sit and slug it out. They had killed their target and they weren't about to let some pain-in-the-ass witness live to tell the tale. He automatically assessed his odds, sure in the knowledge that they would be doing the same thing right at that moment. They didn't look good — for him. He had lost his horse, presumably (they would be bound to think) his ammunition supply and any means of escape. They had Winchesters, as most 'serious' folk did these days, against his Spencer with its three remaining cartridges — though he always kept a couple of spares in his vest. But most important of all, they knew that he was aware that they had bushwhacked the guy — even though he couldn't possibly know who they were, since he had only seen one of them and he was dressed like a scaredy-crow. The fact that they were prepared to kill him meant that they were determined not to be found out as the killers of the man lying down on the gully bottom.

Another couple of bullets honed in on his original spot, but he refrained from returning fire, edging his way backwards rather than moving laterally. Then bullets started spraying the area, as he expected they would. And they started getting too close for comfort, so that he was forced through self-preservation to release a couple of shots with the Spencer in the hope of a lucky shot.

But there was no lucky shot; the fire kept coming from both directions, pinning him down in the tangle of greasewood. He pushed the spare cartridges into the rifle. There was no doubt about it, it was a stacked deck and the hand that he had drawn looked like being a dead man's hand.

Yet Mallory was a true gambling man and he knew that though the cards were bad, if he played them well enough, he could possibly get out of this scrape. It was a slim chance, but if he could play the bluff he could maybe stay in the game a bit longer. At least long enough, Lady Luck willing, to take one of the murdering bastards out with him.

A stray bullet tore up ground in front of his face and he screamed loudly, letting off the Colt as he rolled furiously as far right as he could. He hoped that he might just give the impression that he had been hit and reflexively discharged a shot.

His bluff was to play possum.

The shooting stopped for a couple of minutes then he heard a whistle. Could they have bought it? How long would he have to wait before they decided to check the kill? Minutes dragged by, then another whistle.

From the thicket over on the left a

man appeared. It was the hooded duster coat again. He edged out with his rifle poised at his shoulder, then swiftly started zigzagging from tree to tree.

Immediately, his fellow assailant started firing into Mallory's thicket again. Clearly they were planning to take as few chances as possible.

Mallory took a bead on the tree that the duster coat was hiding behind. Just a little nearer, he thought. One clear shot and maybe, just maybe he could even the odds.

More covering fire rang out, and then duster coat made a fresh dash for another tree. But before he reached it, Mallory let off a shot which missed, but which hit the tree he was running to and sent splinters flying in the face of the running man.

'Damn!' grunted Mallory levering another cartridge into the chamber of the Spencer. But before he could fire, indeed before the echo of his shot had more than faded in his ears, another rifle barked from somewhere behind and above him, kicking up dirt around the feet of the duster-coated rifleman who stared bewilderedly about him then dived for the cover of the tree.

A cold shiver ran up Mallory's spine. Who was this extra gun? Another bushwhacker? He craned his neck round and saw the glint of the sun reflecting from the barrel of a rifle up on top of the gully rim. As he watched, the gun spat angrily four times, two shots at the duster coat and two shots at the other gun, who had clearly honed in on him. Mallory watched the battle that had now switched from him to the point on the rimrock behind him. It was with a feeling of relief and some satisfaction that he saw the guy up above was having the best of it. Duster coat made a sudden retreat with bullets kicking up dust about his feet, literally hurling himself into the trees to escape from the deadly shower. The unknown rifleman kept up his barrage on both positions for a few moments, until it was obvious that his fire was no longer being returned. Then there was the sound of horses retreating. Mallory stayed where he was, caution telling him to bide his time.

A hand holding the rifle vertically appeared over the rimrock and waved. Then a few moments later he heard the sound of another horse moving along behind the edge of the gully rim, until it too had receded into the distance.

Gingerly, Mallory stood up, working his cramped, aching muscles to get the circulation going. He was relieved to see that the roan had not strayed far but seemed to be contentedly grazing on clumps of grass.

On the gully floor the body of the man lay pinned under the corpse of his mount, while high up in the sky, a brace of buzzards, having sensed death and newly shed blood, hovered on air currents awaiting an easy meal. Mallory shuddered at the thought of those beaks and talons indiscriminately ripping flesh from man and horse. He would of course go down and cover the horse up as best he could, then take the man's body into Pasco Springs. But first, it being easier to skirt round to the trees on the opposite incline he decided to see if the bushwhackers had left any debris.

It took him a good ten minutes to circle through the trees and find the first spot, where duster coat had been. The ground was well trodden and littered with empty shells and at least half a dozen smoked-down quirlies. He pocketed a couple of the shells, then made his way through the trees to the second vantage point where a similar patch of detritus greeted him. It had been a planned bushwhacking.

Mallory looked down at the dead horse and rider on the gully floor. They were lying in the middle of a trail that obviously met up with the trail he himself had been coming down. Then he looked back at the point on the rimrock where the other rifleman had joined in. 'Lucky for me he was passing,' he thought, as he began to make his way down to the scene of the crime. 'Yet why had he skedaddled? Maybe he was just shy.' He grinned despite himself. 'A regular shy Good Samaritan!'

By the time he got down to the bottom of the gully blowflies had started to collect around the congealed blood that had oozed out of a wound plumb in the middle of the horse's head, explaining all too clearly how the man had come to be pinned under the mount. The horse had literally died in its tracks as a carefully aimed Winchester bullet had drilled into its brain.

Mallory winced at the sight of the splattering of blood and equine brain on the man's clothes. His eye took in the Peacemaker lying on the ground beside the unmoving hand, the blood-soaked sleeve. He surveyed the unshaved, alabaster white face of a man in his mid-forties. He was heavily jowled and a tad overweight. Then he saw the star pinned to his chest. 'A sheriff, huh? That could explain some.'

A gurgling noise came from the man's throat, causing Tom's eyebrows to shoot up in alarm. He had assumed that the man was long dead, so he swiftly laid his ear to the man's chest, and heard the lub-dub of a slowly beating heart. Then he noticed that blood was still oozing from the wound. 'Hang on, Sheriff,' he urged the unconscious man. 'I'm going to get you to a doctor just as soon as I can. After all this I ain't about to let you die on me. We'll show those murdering bastards.'

2

It was almost two hours later before Mallory reached the south end of the township of Pasco Springs. He had done his best to staunch the sheriff's bleeding chest wound, then hoisted him into the saddle in such a way that he lay along the roan's powerful neck. Then, with his Spencer primed and held in readiness, he had walked the roan the remaining miles into town. Throughout it all the sheriff remained unconscious and silent except for the occasional groan when the roan hit a rut and he was jolted.

A couple of stray dogs greeted him, followed by a gaggle of wide-eyed urchins and a few adult loafers. 'Got a wounded sheriff here,' he announced to an ancient and a young boy who struck an excited pace alongside him. 'I'd appreciate it if'n you'd point me at the town doctor. If you have one, that is.'

'Jezus! It's Dan Milburn, right enough,' the old-timer puffed. 'He ain't croaked, has he mister?'

'Not yet,' Mallory replied, coaxing the roan to follow the gesticulating youngster who had taken off ahead of him. 'Can't say that I care for the folks that hang about outside your town,' he said to the old-timer over his shoulder. 'Two of them bushwhacked the sheriff and damn near did for me as well.'

A fair crowd had gathered by the time they passed up the main street, a mix of clapperboard wood-framed buildings and white-walled adobe fronts. Mallory drew to a halt outside a two-storied building with a sign above the door, proclaiming:

Dr William Hawkins, Physician, Surgeon, Embalmer.

The door opened before Mallory reached the hitching rail and a tall bespectacled man with thinning hair and stooped shoulders came out. He squinted in the failing light, took in the scene and immediately issued orders to a couple of men in the crowd. 'Bring him in real gentle, boys. I can't tell till I examine him lying down, but from here I'd say he's lost more than enough blood.' Then to Mallory: 'You see what happened, stranger?'

Tom pointed to the gouged-out chunk on his saddle horn. 'That's how close they were to unseating me. Bushwhackers! Two of them. I came along just as one of the jaspers, a feller in a duster coat and hood, was about to blow him to kingdom come. I reckon they'd been waiting for him. Then when I showed up they tried to give me the same one-way ticket.'

'How come they let you go?' came a voice from the crowd.

Tom decided to say nothing about his unknown rescuer. Instead, he patted the stock of the Spencer. 'I dissuaded them,' he said meaningly, raising a few guffaws from the crowd. 'The cowardly dogs hightailed it somewheres.'

Doc Hawkins gazed appraisingly at

Mallory for a moment as he let the men pass with the wounded sheriff. 'This will take some time,' he said. 'Why don't you settle down somewhere, have some food then call back and see me. Meanwhile I'll see what I can do for Dan here. Say an hour.'

Tom adjusted his hat and remounted the roan. 'Food sounds good, Doc. But before that me and my mount here could do with some water.'

'Water is something we are fortunate to have plenty of here in Pasco Springs. Go down the main street and you'll come to Reardon's Livery. Tell Rusty I sent you for some of his sweet water.' And with a curt nod he disappeared inside.

Pasco Springs was much like any other cattle and mining town in the south-west. The main street consisted of a bank and assay office, two or three saloon-cum-hotels, an assortment of stores, a sheriff's office and jail, and a telegraph post. Several streets led off it, one to the railyard with its huge water-stack, penyard and feeding boxes. Other streets led to the decent end of town where the self-styled decent citizens lived in their picket-fenced properties clustered around the town church. Yet others led to other parts of the town, where none of the decent folk admitted to going. At least, not to their wives.

As Mallory rode down the street, the crowd gradually dispersed with much mumbling and gossiping, to spread news of the wounded sheriff to the curious faces that looked out from stores and street doorways. Tom dismounted in front of the livery stable and walked the roan through the stout wooden doors to find about a dozen other horses already settled in various boxes. From out back he could hear the noise of hammer on iron, followed by the quenching of hot metal in a bosh water trough, accompanied by an unmelodic song containing enough cuss words to make a mule-skinner blush. The owner of the voice, sixty if he was a day, face tanned like a chestnut, with a grizzled beard, bald pate and farrier's leather apron, looked up on sensing his presence.

'Well now,' said the worthy, laying aside his tongs and hammer on his range, and taking in Tom's grazes and scratches. 'You been in some war, mister?'

'Sort of,' replied Tom. 'I just brought your town sheriff in, all shot up.'

'He daid?'

Tom shook his head. 'I left him at the doctor's place. He's got a couple of holes in him, but I'd lay odds that he'll pull through.'

The liveryman grinned at him with a twinkle in his eye. 'I'm guessing you're a gambling man. A professional.'

Tom returned the grin, taking an instant liking to the livery owner. 'You'd be right, friend. But how come you knew that.'

The other let his head back and guffawed. 'Well now, fancy dudes, a real mix of belongings, a Texas rig saddle,' he gestured at the brace of guns in their holsters, 'Twin Navies and an old Spencer. All spells out someone who accumulates things as he goes along. This part of the world that marks you out as either a thief, which'n you don't look like at all, or a gambling man.'

Again, his eyes twinkled mischievously. 'You sure don't look like any doctor, so I figure that your assessment of the sheriff's wound is more gambling opinion than medical know-how. Anyways mister,' he said extending his hand, 'I'm Rusty, what can I do for you?'

Tom took the man's gnarled, callused hand. 'Mallory, Tom Mallory,' he introduced himself. 'I'd appreciate a box and feed for my horse.'

Rusty pointed to a free box. 'Help yourself, Tom. Fine horseflesh,' he remarked with professional interest. 'Someone take a shot at you?' He examined the wound on the horse's rump. 'Four more days,' he pronounced matter-of-factly, 'then it'll be healed up so's you won't notice.'

Tom began unbuckling his saddle. 'Five will get you ten, it'll take six days.'

Rusty guffawed heartily, spat in his palm and held his hand out to shake. 'A bet it is, but this is one you'll sure lose, Tom. Horse healing I know about.'

Tom set about tending to the roan. 'This sheriff of yours, is he well liked?'

'Dan Milburn? Not exactly liked. In fact for most of the time he's been sheriff I guess people haven't noticed him. He was partial to a drink, a lot of drink. Until the lynching, that is. Then he seemed to take his job a tad more serious. Guilt I guess.' He hefted an armload of hay into the box for the roan, then continued. 'Maybe he took his job a bit too serious after that. Bushwhacking a sheriff ain't an everyday occurrence if you ask me.'

Having sorted his mount out, Tom turned his attention to his own needs. 'The doc said I should tell you that he sent me, and that I should ask you for some of Pasco Springs' sweet water.'

Rusty laughed and pointed through the back to the water pump. 'Help yourself, Tom, wash off some of that trail dust and treat your tonsils. It's the only thing we can be proud of, our sweet water. Which is more'n can be said for the range outside town. This summer has dried up some of the creeks and caused more'n a bit of bad feeling among the ranchers. Some say that water's been the cause of that lynching, never mind no rape.'

Tom went through and pumped a stream of water and sluiced his face, wincing as it stung some of the grazes. 'About this lynching,' he said over his shoulder as he straightened up.

Then he felt a gun barrel stuck in the small of his back, followed by the cocking of its hammer. 'One move and you're a dead man,' growled a voice directly behind him.

'Hey! No gunplay in my livery,' Rusty protested angrily.

'Keep out of this, Rusty,' purred another smoother voice from a few feet behind. 'Now you mister, put your hands up slowly and turn around.'

Tom acquiesced. 'Friendly town you have here,' he said with an innocent smile. Yet despite the smile his mind rapidly registered the presence of four men. The gunman directly in front of him was dressed in range clothes that were neat and clean, devoid of evidence of work. The hand that held the gun was steady in a tight-fitting glove. The face clean-shaven, sharp featured and handsome, but for dark cruel eyes. Beside him was another rangeman, shorter and altogether grubbier. And behind them was the smooth-talker, a slickly dressed man of average height, smelling slightly of cologne. Beside him was a short, portly man with a spade-like beard that barely disguised a permanently pained expression, a result, Tom guessed, of whatever condition caused him to need the stick that he leaned so heavily upon.

'We're a decent town, mister,' said the smooth-talker. 'We just don't take kindly to our sheriff being brought in wounded by somebody we don't know squat about.'

'And what authority do you have for holding a gun on me?' Tom asked.

'We're the town's — er — senior citizens,' returned the man, only to look askance at Rusty, as the liveryman snorted in seeming derision. Tom watched as Rusty made his way back to the tools at the forge.

'I'm Tyler Kent, the owner of the Four Kings Saloon, the town's premier hotel and saloon,' went on the smooth-talker. 'My friend here is Mr Chester Harrington, our banker and assayer. And these gentlemen, Mr Wheeler and Mr Jarvis are upstanding citizens of our locality.'

'Yeah,' sneered Jarvis, the grubby rangeman. 'And we don't like bush-whacking drifters.'

'Harsh words, mister,' said Tom, eyeing the man distastefully.

'Like I said stranger,' went on Kent, the saloon owner, 'we care for our own.

Now prove that you had no hand in the shooting of Dan Milburn.'

'Easy enough,' Tom replied. 'You just have to ask the sheriff when he recovers. He saw the two men who attacked him.'

There was the sound of footsteps at the entrance of the livery stable. 'We won't be able to ask Dan anything,' came Doc Hawkins' voice. 'He just died ten minutes ago. There was nothing I could do for him. It looks like we have a murder here in Pasco Springs.'

Everyone, including Tom, looked stunned at the news. He had known that the sheriff was badly wounded, but he'd seen men pull through with worse-looking wounds and more blood loss.

'Shuck that gunbelt real slow,' ordered Wheeler, the gunman, prodding the barrel of his weapon into Tom's abdomen.

Tom's jaw muscles tensed momentarily. He was conscious that the livery entrance was now crowded with people who had gathered, presumably upon hearing the news about the sheriff and the man who had brought him in. Now a murmur of gossip and discontent was emanating from the crowd as they watched this new drama unfold. He felt his brow grow clammy, yet he was not one to panic.

He slowly undid the buckle and held his belt out. The gunman nodded for Jarvis to take it, which he seemed to do with extraordinary relish.

'This is a big mistake,' said Tom. 'I didn't shoot your sheriff. I came across two jaspers just as they were about to finish him off. They'd already taken his horse down and disabled him.'

'Can you prove this?' asked Chester Harrington, speaking for the first time.

Tom turned his head to the doctor. 'Did you dig a bullet out of him, Doc?'

Doc Hawkins tapped his waistcoat pocket. 'Uh huh, I extracted a bullet from his chest. I have it right here.'

'My guess is it's a .45.'

The doctor drew out the slug and

nodded, holding it in his palm for the others to see.

'In my vest pocket I reckon I've probably got a case that it could have come out of. At any rate a .45 case.'

Tyler Kent dipped his fingers into Tom's vest pocket and drew out a couple of the shells. He took the bullet from the doctor and slid a shell over it. 'OK, it's a .45 slug and .45 shells. So what does this tell us, mister?'

Tom smiled. 'Look at my rifle and you'll see that it's a Spencer, which uses a .52.' He nodded towards his gunbelt. 'And my Navy Colts fire a .36.'

Chester Harrington had drawn the Spencer from its scabbard and sniffed it. 'A Spencer, all right, but it's been fired.'

'I had a run-in myself with the bushwhackers,' Tom explained, outlining what had happened, yet for a reason he was himself unsure of, again omitted mention of the unknown rescuer. 'When I went scouting their positions I found these empty shells. My guess is that you'll also find that the bullets in the sheriff's horse are .45s.'

Chester Harrington frowned. 'And just how could you know that?'

'The sounds,' said Tom. 'It's a slight difference, I'll allow, but it's a clear difference.'

Doc Hawkins pursed his lips and nodded. 'It all sounds plausible to me. We don't know about the bullets in Dan Milburn's horse, but that one that I removed from Dan himself, may he rest in peace, is certainly a .45. There is no way that this gentleman could have shot him. I suggest we give Mr — '

'Mallory, Tom Mallory.'

'I suggest we give Mr Mallory his guns back,' the doctor said.

All this while Wheeler the gunman had been staring straight at Tom's eyes, his gunhand as steady as a rock. Now with a shrug he deftly returned his gun to its holster, then held out his hand to his companion for Tom's gunbelt. He took a step closer to Tom, his lips drawing back over his teeth in a leer that was less than friendly. 'Seem to know a lot about guns, don't you, Pilgrim!'

One or two murmurs rose from among the few faces that had remained at the livery entrance. Many had drifted away when the drama seemed to subside. Now it looked as if it might build up again as Wheeler, a man with a reputation as something of a hard man, continued to assert himself.

Tom smiled back innocently. 'Some.'

Wheeler lifted Tom's gunbelt admiringly. 'Mighty fine stitchwork, smooth, soft leather. Twin Navies. Looks like they may've seen a bit of action.'

Jarvis guffawed. 'Girlie guns, if'n you ask me.'

Tom looked at the grubby rangeman and his smile deepened. 'If you say so. I can see that you are the sort of dashing fellow who would draw girls to him like a candle draws moths.'

A few titters came from the doorway. Conflict was always a welcome entertainment for town loafers, as long as they weren't themselves involved in it.

'You some kinda comedian?' barked Jarvis.

'Some,' replied Tom, without letting the smile slip.

Wheeler's handsome face also broke into a smile. 'That's it, Pilgrim,' he said soothingly, winking aside at Jarvis. 'Enjoy your joke at my friend's expense. Just remember that he's the sort who holds grudges.' His hand tightened over the handle of one of the Navy Colts and drew it slowly from its holster.

'Now that ain't polite,' Tom said, the grin still playing over his lips. 'Didn't anyone ever tell you not to toy with another man's gun?'

And before anyone was aware of it, Wheeler's own gun was in Tom's hand, the barrel pressed against his belly and the hammer noisily clicked back. Only then did Tom's smile fade and his eyes narrow. 'Now put the gun back in the holster and buckle it back on me.'

Jarvis swore and took a step closer,

his right hand hovering above his Peacemaker. Then he swore again, but this time in pain as Rusty rapped his knuckles with a pair of tongs. As Jarvis clutched his hand in pain Rusty slid the rangeman's weapon from its holster and tossed it backwards into a heap of horse dung. 'I said no gunplay in my livery,' he said with grated teeth. Then, turning to Tom: 'But I appreciate that a man's gotta get his own possessions back. You carry on, Tom.'

Wheeler glared at Rusty before returning his gaze to Tom. 'Go to hell!'

Tom pressed the barrel half an inch harder. 'Do it! Now!'

The man's face suffused with choked-back rage, but he did as he was bidden, then stepped back a pace. Tom uncocked the weapon, twirled it once as he leaned over to let it drop into the other's holster. As he rose the smile flashed back to his face. 'And you remember this, my friend — the name's Mallory. Don't call me Pilgrim again.'

Wheeler glowered hatred at Tom.

'We're going to meet again,' he said, signalling Jarvis, who retrieved his gun from the dung heap with a malevolent glare at Rusty. They pushed their way unceremoniously through the few grinning stragglers who had determinedly stayed in the hope of seeing some sort of action.

When they had gone Chester Harrington held out his hand. 'No hard feelings, Mallory. We're all a bit edgy lately and we can't be too careful.' Tom shook his hand good-humouredly. 'We're also somewhat vulnerable now that Sheriff Milton has been murdered,' the bearded banker went on. 'And we have an unprotected bank.'

Tom pursed his lips. 'Then I guess I'll need to be calling on you tomorrow, Mr Harrington. I have some business I'll need to run by you. I've just come into possession of the deed of a ranch,' said Tom. 'The Diamond T.'

For some reason the little banker's face drained of colour.

3

Jeremiah Ignatius Reardon, one time corporal in the US Army, overland Concord driver turned farrier, blacksmith and liveryman, known to all and sundry in Pasco Springs as Rusty, chewed tobacco and handled the reins of his buckboard team with genuine skill. Tom Mallory sat by his side puffing furiously on a cheroot to mask the smell emanating from the horse's carcass behind them.

It was not long after sun-up and they had driven out to collect Dan Milburn's dead mount. Tom had accepted Rusty's offer of overnight hospitality, which had involved a few rounds of cards, some acceptable antelope stew and more whiskey than Tom usually cared for. When Rusty rousted him in the morning full of the joys of spring, Tom realized that liquor was no stranger to the liveryman.

Before they winched it up onto the buckboard Tom had dug out two slugs from the horse, one from the chest and one from its cranium. He showed them to the liveryman, who identified them as being .45s. 'You sure you didn't see anything that might identify those murdering bastards?' Rusty asked.

Tom had taken to the older man who had helped him out the day before, and whose hospitality and hard-earned dollars he had enjoyed. He decided that he could trust him enough to tell him about the unknown extra hand.

Rusty shook his head. 'Don't make much sense, Tom. Why wouldn't this *hombre* show hisself?'

Tom blew out a slow stream of blue smoke. 'Seems there are a lot of mysteries round here, Rusty.'

To Tom's amazement Rusty began to laugh. 'Talking of mysteries, Tom, I'm willing to bet that Frank Wheeler is trying to puzzle out who the hell you are to humiliate him like you did yesterday evening. I can still see his face when you snook his own gun on him.' He slapped his knee and dissolved into good-natured mirth. 'Where'd you learn to draw another man's gun so fast?'

Tom ignored the question, substituting one of his own. 'What's his place in Pasco Springs, Rusty? He didn't exactly look the part of an upstanding citizen as that Kent dude said. He looked like a man who fancies his ability with guns.'

Rusty spat contemptuously. 'Bully boy gunnie, that's what he is. Him and that rat Ben Jarvis are both Bar W men. In fact, Frank Wheeler is old Sam Wheeler's very own nephew, sorta heir to the spread, I guess. He's supposed to be the foreman and that Jarvis is his *segundo*, though they both seem to spend more time in town than they do at the Bar W.'

'I assumed that they worked for Tyler Kent,' mused Tom.

Rusty shrugged his shoulders. 'Maybe they do in an unofficial capacity. Certainly drink enough at his place and I guess they do him little favours.'

'Is Kent as important as he thinks?'

'Likes to think he is. Sure has amassed a passel o' wealth. Owns the Four Kings Saloon, an emporium and seems to have his fingers in quite a few pies round the area.'

Tom smoked in silence for a few moments, then asked: 'So this Sam Wheeler, what sort of cove is he?'

'A tough old bird,' replied Rusty. 'He and his young brother were the first ranchers in these parts. Fought off apaches, built up the Bar W over the years, then Cal, that was the younger brother, got hisself consumption and died. His wife followed soon after and old Sam brought up their kid, Frank Wheeler. Now the Bar W is the biggest outfit in the valley. It's about twice the size of your'n.'

Tom drew meditatively on his cheroot. 'Strange business. I win the Diamond T in a card game from a young redheaded punter, then I ride towards Pasco Springs straight into a bushwhacking.'

'That redheaded youngster would be Jeff Trent, old Jake Trent's son. Redheaded, just like his paw — God rest his soul.'

'And you started to tell me last night about him being lynched.'

Rusty spat out his wad of tobacco, as if he had suddenly lost the taste for it. He pulled out a flask and proffered it to Tom, who declined, before taking a hefty swig.

'Damned dirty business, Tom. The whole town seemed to go crazy — got all fired up on free booze at the Four Kings then broke into the jail. The deputy, a bar-dog name of Burnett high-tailed it outta the back door and left them to it.'

'Where was the sheriff?'

'Drunk somewhere, I guess. Dan Milburn warn't much of a lawman, till then. Afterwards though, well he seemed to get serious.' He took another swig of tonsil paint and noisily sucked air in between his teeth as the liquor hit the spot. 'I reckon he started poking his nose in where it wasn't appreciated.'

'What did this Trent guy do?'

'Raped and strangled a girl, they said. One of Lucinda Grey's gals. She didn't live in the Longbow, but had her own place, a little shack down behind the telegraph office. Tyler Kent and a couple of his regulars say they saw him coming outta her place that night. Looked kinda panicked, they said.'

'Which he naturally would do if'n he did it.'

Rusty let out a string of cuss words. 'No way did he do it, Tom. Jake Trent was a decent type. Why would a guy like him have to go visit a young girl when he had a brand new wife at home? Especially when she looked as good as Nell Trent.'

Tom lit another cheroot. 'So Nell Trent is this Jeff Trent's stepmother?'

Rusty nodded. 'Yeh, but she's maybe only a year or two older than him.' He took a final swig and pocketed his flask. 'And I'm guessing she ain't gonna be too happy to find the ranch handed over to some — no offence, Tom — some tinhorn gambler. Truth is that she's been more or less running the Diamond T. Since the lynching Jeff has pretty well spent his time diving to the bottom of a bottle.'

So the Diamond T had a young widow holding the reins, Tom thought. Things just seemed to be getting more and more complicated.

* * *

Chester Harrington's office at the back of the First Bank of Pasco Springs reflected the personality of the man. It was neat, uncluttered, and businesslike. The single small window was barred and let in an adequate amount of light through its opaque smoked glass. A man-sized safe stood in the corner of the room surrounded by shelves which seemed to groan under the weight of rows of even, neatly labelled ledgers. A single painting hung on the wall behind the huge oak desk, which was itself devoid of clutter, bearing only a single file, an inkstand, cigar box and a large ashtray.

When Tom Mallory was ushered in by the bank's chief teller he fancied that he saw a guilty flush spread over the banker's cheeks, as he hurriedly stowed a small box in a drawer of the desk.

After initial pleasantries Chester Harrington proffered the cigar box. Tom selected a cigar and produced flame for them both to light their smokes.

'Well, down to business,' said the banker, opening the file, which Tom could see contained documents and letters relating to the Diamond T ranch. 'Have you been out to see your property yet, Mr Mallory?'

Tom blew out a stream of smoke. 'Not yet. You said yesterday that the ranch owed the bank money. Figured I'd best see what sort of hand I've drawn first before I show my cards at the ranch.'

The banker tugged at his prodigious beard as he contemplated the end of his cigar. 'If you'll take my advice you won't leave it too long, Mr Mallory. It's bound to come as a shock to Mrs Trent that she is no longer the mistress of the ranch.'

Then the banker grasped his cigar between his teeth and turned to a page bearing an itemized column of neat numbering, with a total figure underlined. This was followed by a dated agreement of loan written in the same copperplate style. It was signed by Chester Harrington, obviously the scribe of the agreement, and by Jake Trent.

Despite himself Tom's eyebrows shot up and he whistled. 'Twelve thousand dollars! That's more than I have readily available.'

The banker sat forward and cleared his throat as he turned the ledger back towards himself. 'I was worried about that, Mr Mallory.' A thin smile hovered over his lips. 'Of course, if you decided to cut your losses, I'm sure that I could find a buyer who would make you an offer. Enough to clear the debt to the bank and still turn you a handsome profit.'

But Tom shook his head and stood up. He smiled and held out his hand. 'Like you said, Mr Harrington, I need to have a look at my ranch first.'

The banker had risen stiffly, supporting himself with a hand on the desk. 'Just don't take too long deciding, Mr Mallory,' he returned, a slight edge having crept into his voice. 'The bank can allow some leeway over the loan, at my discretion, but the due date for return of the loan is well nigh imminent.'

Once outside the bank Tom grinned to himself. Someone wanted the Diamond T and one thing was clear — whoever it was, they had the little banker in their pocket.

* * *

Tom followed Rusty into the Longbow saloon and let the batwing doors flap closed behind him as he stood surveying the interior. It was early evening and the place was lit up by half a dozen oil lamps, strategically placed near long mirrors to give maximum illumination where it was needed and wanted, yet allow other parts to languish in the half-shadow required by those saloon users who desired discretion with their drinking.

The floor was scrubbed, devoid of sawdust, the bar neatly polished, and the tables and chairs of a superior quality to the usual saloon in the south-west.

All told, the hand of a woman was evident. A piano player was pounding out a lively air, which had successfully induced a few customers to venture onto the dance floor with brightly clad saloon girls. And already men were playing faro, monte and poker at the green baize-topped tables in the playing area.

'Lo Rusty,' greeted the portly bald barkeep.

'Hi Curly,' returned Rusty. 'Me and my friend here'll risk a coupla your beers. Preferably the ones without the extra water this time.'

Curly winked good-humouredly at Tom as he began pouring frothing beer into pristine clean glasses. 'Enjoy your drink, boyos,' he said sliding the drinks towards them. 'But this time how about paying with proper coin, not that stuff you turn out on that forge of yours.'

The three men laughed and joked for a few minutes, until a door at the back of the bar opened and Tom stopped and stared with his glass half-raised to his lips. The woman who entered would have caused most men to pause. Her raven-black hair, full lips and olive skin hinted at some Hispanic blood. In a flame-coloured dress that showed off her feminine charms to perfection, she came towards the trio with a smile that displayed perfect white teeth.

Rusty poked Tom in the ribs causing him to spill beer, which mercifully also released him from the woman's spell. Rusty chuckled. 'Lucinda, come meet my friend Tom.' And turning to Tom, he introduced: 'Mrs Lucinda Grey, owner of the best saloon in Pasco Springs.'

'I heard about your welcome to Pasco Springs yesterday, Tom.'

'Yeh, I reckon I upset a couple of the locals.' He winked at Rusty. 'With a little help from my friend here.'

Rusty wiped beer froth from his whiskers. 'Allus happy to even odds,' he said. 'Never could stand seeing two agin' one.'

'Which is how it was with the sheriff, I understand,' said Lucinda. 'Until you came along.'

At that very moment a girl screamed and a commotion broke out over on the dance floor. A drunken cowboy was getting too fresh with one of the dance girls and was swinging one fist threateningly at a couple of customers who were noisily remonstrating with him. And then Curly appeared on the dance floor, a veritable whirlwind despite his portly bulk. He simply pitched in under the cowboy's flailing arm, grabbed him by the scruff of the neck and frog-marched him through the batwing doors. He reappeared a moment afterwards, a few beads of perspiration on his forehead being the only indication that anything untoward had occurred.

Lucinda gave a short melodic laugh. 'As you can see we have no truck with folks who try to cut up rough. Curly O'Toole has the Irish sense of justice and I've yet to see him fail to eject an unwanted customer.' She flashed a lovely smile at him then headed off to mingle with her customers.

Rusty finished his drink then left Tom, who searched out a corner table where he began to play solitaire. From time to time he found himself looking across at Lucinda Grey as she moved hither and thither among her clientele, laughing and joking with them all.

About half an hour later Tom saw Chester Harrington hobble in with an older man with an iron-grey moustache and a severe case of weather-beaten wrinkles. Behind them were three armed men: the two men Tom had tangled with the previous evening,

Frank Wheeler and the leering Ben Jarvis, and a tall skinny youngster with a heavily pock-marked face. Harrington tugged the sleeve of the older man's jacket and pointed in Tom's direction.

'Mr Mallory, this is Sam Wheeler, owner of the Bar W,' the banker introduced.

The rancher's handshake was firm and curt, exactly the same as the man himself. 'I'd like to talk business with you, Mr Mallory. You've got a ranch that I want to buy.'

Tom lit a cheroot and gestured to a chair. 'Actually, I'm not in a good business mood right now,' he said. 'I'm in a gambling mood, that's why you find me right here in this saloon. How about a little game.'

Harrington the banker predictably raised his hands. 'I never gamble.'

But Sam Wheeler sat down and drew out a wad of notes from his wallet. 'Just you and me then,' said the rancher. He signalled to Curly and a fresh deck of cards was duly brought across by one of the girls, a pretty brunette.

For the next few minutes there was little talk, except for the raising of bets and the calling of hands. A few dollars passed each way. Then, draining his glass, Sam Wheeler said: 'OK, Mr Mallory, we've played your game, now how about it. I want to buy the Diamond T and I'm willing to pay a good price.'

Tom sat back and savoured his cigar. 'Trouble is I just can't say what a fair price is. I haven't seen the ranch yet.'

Wheeler jerked a thumb over his shoulder to where the banker was sipping a drink at the bar. 'Chester Harrington will tell you exactly what the ranch is worth. I'll pay the price he asks, no question.'

Tom pursed his lips. 'Somehow I can't understand all this haste,' he said between puffs on his cigar. 'First Mr Harrington and now you.'

Sam Wheeler bristled. 'Now see here . . . '

But he did not finish, because a

gloved hand slammed a riding quirt on the table. Sam Wheeler looked up and found himself staring at the personification of beautiful anger. A young woman of about twenty-six with straw-blonde hair and the most exquisitely fine, fair features was standing over him. She was dressed in a riding dress with high boots and a hat hanging down her back. Just behind her stood a stocky weather-beaten man in range clothes.

'You worm, Sam Wheeler! First my husband and now his son. If I was a man I'd whip you within an inch of your life.'

To his credit Sam Wheeler sat unmoved. 'I don't know what you're talking about, Mrs Trent. I had nothing to do with your man's lynching. And I don't know what you're saying about your stepson.'

Tom cleared his throat. 'Actually, ma'am, I have a hunch that your stepson will turn up real soon.'

Cold, smouldering eyes turned on him. 'He already has come home,' she said, her voice quaking with barely concealed ire. 'He told me all about losing the ranch to a professional gambler. That I imagine is you! And just when were you deigning to visit your ranch?' She looked contemptuously from Tom to Sam Wheeler. 'I suppose you had to report to your boss first.'

Tom was about to remonstrate, but was beaten to it by Sam Wheeler. 'You know, the name of Trent is getting mighty unpopular in these parts lately.'

'Yeah boss, maybe the whole area would be better off without a murdering rapist's family,' the pock-marked youth piped up.

In a single bound the stocky cowboy attending Nell Trent had crossed the space between them and punched the youth full in the face. A spray of blood was followed by the sound of a tooth hitting the floor. Almost instantly chairs were scraping backwards as the Longbow patrons either made to get out of the way, or strove to get a better view.

But the sudden explosion of a shotgun being discharged ceiling-wise, followed by a descending shower of falling plaster and wood splinters froze everyone into inactivity.

'That's enough! If you want to fight, do it outside!' Lucinda Grey cried forcefully, standing beside Curly O'Toole, who held a smoking sawn-off shotgun all too visibly in his hands. After a few moments' silence the piano player started up again and people slowly returned to their groups at the bar and gaming tables.

Lucinda swept across to Tom's table, where Nell Trent stood glaring at Sam Wheeler. 'Satisfied?' Lucinda asked the young widow.

Nell Trent shook her head. 'All I want is my husband's ranch back.'

'The hell you do!' spat Sam Wheeler. 'I'm about to buy it.'

Tom Mallory grinned despite himself. 'Appears to me everyone wants this ranch, so I propose a simple and speedy solution.' He held up the pack of cards. 'A three-way cut. Lady Luck decides.'

4

A crowd gathered round the table as the clientele of the Longbow sensed that the drama was not yet played out.

'Aces High — three-way cut,' Tom announced. 'If Mr Wheeler wins he gets to buy the ranch from me. Mrs Trent wins and she gets to keep the Diamond T, but gives me a steak a day until I decide to hoist leather.'

'And if you win?' Nell Trent demanded, her brow beetling in consternation. 'Don't you think for one minute that I'm part of the ranch furnishings.'

Tom laughed. 'No, ma'am. If I win I keep the ranch, but you and your stepson stay on to help me run it. No strings attached.' He took the cards, executed a waterfall shuffle, and then pushed the deck towards Nell Trent.

She pursed her lips, hesitated for a few moments, then cut the deck. She smiled, 'Queen of Hearts.'

Tom nodded to Sam Wheeler, who cut the Four of Clubs. The rancher scowled. 'I don't know what your game is, Mallory . . . '

'Gambling!' replied Tom with a grin. 'I let Lady Luck decide what's going to happen.' And with apparent disinterest he leaned forward and cut the deck to reveal the King of Diamonds. 'Well now, my favourite one-eyed King. Looks like I win and have myself a lady ranch manager.'

Sam Wheeler scraped his chair back and stood up. 'I'm a patient man, Mallory. But I'm a determined man. My next offer may not be as generous as you would like.' Saying which, he swept out of the Longbow followed by his entourage.

'Congratulations, Mr Mallory,' said Nell Trent, coldly. 'I'll expect you at the ranch soon. But as I said, I'm no part of the deal except as the ranch manager.' Then she too flounced out of the saloon followed by her foreman.

It was then that Tom and Lucinda realized that they shared a love of excitement. Once the crowd had drifted away with much gleeful muttering and hoots of pleasure that would be the focus for conversation all evening, they retired to one of the saloon's secluded corners. There over a couple of drinks Lucinda confided: 'I love gambling but I only ever gamble when I like the size of the pot.'

'In that case does the lady care to ante?'

'You bet,' she answered with a coquettish smile. 'In fact Tom, I'll raise you.'

⋆ ⋆ ⋆

Lucinda and Tom rolled apart and lay beside each other in Lucinda's brass-frame bed in post-coital delirium. It was about two o'clock and the room was dark save for a shaft of moonlight shining through the open first-floor window.

'Excitement should be your middle name, Tom,' Lucinda whispered, running a finger across his chest. 'Either that or Lunatic! You could have lost the Diamond T and ended up empty-handed.'

'I know,' he replied. 'Real exciting, wasn't it?'

They laughed as they thought about the events of the previous evening, culminating in their passionate love-making. Then as their laughter came to a natural pause Tom asked the inevitable question. 'So is there a Mr Grey?'

'There was. A no-good philanderer who left me near high and dry and ran off with one of the girls.' She shrugged. 'Not that it did him much good. He was caught card-cheating down in Senora.' She turned her dark, beautiful eyes on him challengingly. 'I hate cheats, Tom.'

He laughed and kissed her upturned nose. 'A good gambler has no need to cheat, Lucinda. Poker is an art and most players are quite artless. I earn my living honestly. But what about Pasco Springs, who runs things around here?'

Lucinda laughed, a delicious soft laugh that sent a tremble through his system. 'There are a lot of men who think they run the town, Tom. Tyler Kent owns the Four Kings, an Emporium and a couple of smaller stores. He's always trying to extend his wealth. He's a lady's man. He tried to buy me out at first. Then he tried courting me. Even asked me to marry him.'

Tom raised a quizzical eyebrow. 'But you turned him down?'

'Once bitten, twice shy. Besides, I guess he'd be a hard dog to keep on the porch. He likes women a lot.'

'What about the banker?'

'Chester Harrington? He does his job all right, I suppose. He has a reputation for being a skinflint, so he's in the right profession. Never seen him even look at a woman, he always seems to be in too much pain to think of anything else.'

'Sam Wheeler hasn't cottoned to me,' Tom stated. 'I think he's a man used to getting what he wants.'

'You said it. And the same goes for that slime ball of a nephew of his. He's rode on his uncle's coat-tails for so long I think he thinks he's some sort of royalty.'

'I like the town doctor,' Tom volunteered.

'Doc Hawkins, yes he seems straight. Always seems to have the right pill, potion or new-fangled treatment. And he's good with his hands. He's set more bones and dug out more bullets than any other sawbones I've ever known.'

Tom nodded. 'All in all a pretty average sort of town — except for the lynching!'

Lucinda cast her eyes downwards. 'That was bad, Tom. Real evil. But so was the murder and rape of one of my girls. Betsy-May was a good girl, a bit head-strong, but there was no harm in her.' She bit her lip. 'I wish I'd made her live here.'

'Do you believe the man they lynched did it?'

She shook her head. 'I just don't know, Tom.' She ran a hand over his chest, then: 'You ask a lot of questions, Mr Mallory. Now it's my turn. I told you I was a widow, how about you? Why are you drifting about, winning a ranch in a poker game one day then risking losing it another day in a cut of the cards?'

Tom chuckled, yet without genuine humour. 'I guess I'm also a sorta widow, Lucinda. At least I was almost married. My fiancée died a week before we were due to get married.'

And he recounted how he had been the newly appointed constable in the small Texas cowtown of Dodsville a few years before. He told her of the night he had left her in the constable's office while he did a swift round of the town. And he told her of the stick of dynamite that a former 'client' posted through the window, which had blown the office and his beloved Annabelle into a multitude of pieces.

'Tom, I can't say how sorry I am,'

said Lucinda, raising herself on an elbow.

Tom gave a hollow laugh, kissed her full lips, then rolled out of bed. In a trice he had pulled on his britches and shirt.

'I've got to — '

His words were cut short as a fireball flashed between them and thudded into the wall.

Tom stumbled back staring for a moment at the flaming kerosene-soaked arrow embedded in the wall. Already flames had started crawling up the wall and thick black smoke was billowing out.

He picked up a pitcher from the washstand and doused the arrow, with only partial effect. 'What the hell?' Lucinda cried, jumping from the bed to look out of the window.

'No!' Tom cried.

There was the crack of a rifle and a livid streak of blood appeared on Lucinda's shoulder as she was hurtled backwards.

'Stay put!' Tom barked, as he grabbed the quilt and began smothering the flames. Then he was by her side, kissing her with relief as he saw that her wound was merely a nick, although deep enough to tear muscle and produce a lot of blood.

Beyond the door people were stirring, shouting in alarm and running down corridors after the unexpected noise of gunfire and the dreaded smell of fire. Hysterical knocking at the door and frightened, concerned female voices were hushed by Lucinda's firm command to stay calm and go down to the saloon. Above all this Curly O'Toole's Irish brogue could be heard cursing and mumbling about what he was going to do with his shotgun.

Tom put a finger to his lips and crawled on all fours towards the window. On the way past the bed he collected two pillows. He raised one above his head and immediately there was a gunshot and the pillow exploded in a cloud of eiderdown.

Tom grinned at Lucinda as he reached for his gunbelt and strapped it on. Then grabbing the other pillow he raised himself into a crouch position.

'No Tom!' Lucinda gasped. 'Don't risk it.'

But Tom took no notice. He held the pillow out the window and as it exploded from another shot he dived through the window, rolling on the balcony before springing up and launching himself over the wooden balustrade to land in the dirt behind a stack of beer barrels. Instantly, a gun barked from the alleyway across the street, noisily perforating one of the barrels.

Tom peered through a space and saw, then heard Curly O'Toole run out of the saloon wearing nothing but his long johns, threatening merry hell as he waved his shotgun menacingly. Only this was no saloon situation where he could intimidate an offender. It was night-time and his opponent was hidden. Curly came to the end of the alley, raised his shotgun, then died as a bullet blew the top of his head off. For a moment his body stayed upright, until a reflexive convulsion shook him off his feet and he collapsed backwards, the shotgun discharging spontaneously and peppering the frontage of Tyler Kent's Emporium.

Tom felt a spasm of sorrow over the violent death of the Irishman and vowed to avenge him. Of one thing he was certain, there were two bush-whackers out to get him and they just had to be the same two he'd had dealings with before.

He ventured to push the barrel slightly to one side to improve his view of the other side of the street. But almost simultaneously two guns exploded from the other side, honing in on the gap.

'Bastards!' Tom whispered to himself. 'But at least now I know where you are.'

One was ensconced in the alley Curly had been making for, while the other was nestled behind the side wall of the jailhouse.

The unexpected boom of another shotgun near the jailhouse was followed by Rusty's voice. 'I'll get this bastard,

Tom,' he cried. 'You take the other one.'

And indeed, Tom had already taken advantage of the shotgun explosion to clear the barrels and sprint for the other side of the street, both guns blazing.

Another explosion indicated that Rusty had discharged his second barrel.

Tom flattened himself against the wall of the Emporium and listened. The sound of running feet on dirt alerted him to the retreat of one of the would-be assassins. He moved swiftly, entered the alley and spied a dim shadow running for the far end. He let off three shots, aiming low to try and bring his man down. A cry of pain raised his hopes and he started to run, only to trip and fall headlong into the dirt. As he tried to jump up he realized that his feet were tangled. Feeling down he found his foot snared in the discarded bow that had been used to launch the flaming arrow.

The noise of horse hoofs galloping away brought a curse to his lips — a curse that was echoed forcefully by

Rusty as he and several other townsfolk joined Tom in the alley.

'Murderin' bastards!' spat Rusty. 'They've killed Curly, the best danged saloon-keep we ever had in Pasco Springs.'

Tom holstered his weapons. 'But at least I nicked one of the dogs,' he thought.

* * *

Lucinda squeezed Tom's hand while Doc Hawkins deftly sutured the wound on her shoulder.

'You were lucky my girl,' the doctor remarked, peering through wire-framed spectacles perched on the tip of his nose. 'A few inches east and . . . '

'Don't even think of that, Doc,' Lucinda said with a shiver. 'It's bad enough that they murdered poor Curly.'

The doctor straightened up and sucked air between his teeth. 'Your arm's going to feel real numb for a few days, unless I stimulate the nerves and muscle.' He crossed his consulting room to a table on the far side of his roll-top desk. It was bedecked with strange-looking glass jars full of liquids, rods and copper coils. He selected one with long wires leading from it and returned to the couch.

'The very latest in medicine from back east,' he explained. 'This is a galvanic battery for giving what they call Faradic Stimulation.' He handed Lucinda a rod to hold while he strapped a paddle gently over her upper arm.

'This'll tickle a bit,' he informed her as he twisted wires together on top of the battery. Immediately the muscles on her arm started to twitch so that despite herself, Lucinda giggled.

'Why, it's making my arm move all by itself,' she uttered in amazement.

'This is the future, folks,' said the doctor. 'Copper! These wires transmit electric currents. Back east they have buildings illuminated with electric light.' His eyes twinkled almost reverently, as if he could see this vision of the future.

'One day we'll laugh at our primitive kerosene lamps and simple electric batteries like these.'

Lucinda giggled again. 'I think you'd better turn this tickling machine of yours off now, Doc, or I'm going to pee myself with laughing.'

* * *

Tom had just taken Lucinda back to the Longbow, then returned to the sidewalk for a last cheroot when Rusty collared him. It was still dark and the liveryman was carrying a kerosene lamp and a bucket.

'I looked everywhere for it, Tom. Figured I'd best find it afore some kid or lady stumbled across it in the morning.'

'What?' Tom gasped in exasperation.

'Curly's brain!' Rusty exclaimed. 'Those bastards shot his brain right outta his head. I've been searching for ages, but now I found it. And it ain't pretty, Tom.' For the first time Tom realized that his friend's face didn't just look pale because of the lamplight. Shock had drained his face of colour. In his other hand he held a large jar containing a jelly-like mass of grey-pink pulp attached to a segment of bone and bloody scalp flesh. 'Curly was my friend,' Rusty explained. 'I don't want him to go to Boot Hill unless he's kinda intact.'

Tom tossed his cheroot on the sidewalk and ground his heel on it. He had suddenly lost the taste for it. 'Come on Rusty,' he said. 'Let's take it to the Doc's, and see what he can do.'

Doc Hawkins led them through to his backroom and dismissed Tom's apologies for keeping him from sleep.

'In my profession you get used to catnapping. Besides, it's always as well to get the pieces together as soon as possible after a shooting.'

Curly's body lay on a large metal tray atop a deal table. His lifeless eyes were still open, his face frozen in a curious puzzled expression, made all the more surreal by the loss of the top of his head. Rusty and Tom looked on in fascinated horror as the doctor fished the brain and skull piece out of the jar with long-handled forceps and rinsed it in a basin before fitting it into position like a macabre three-dimensional jigsaw. Hawkins pursed his lips and nodded pensively. 'I should be able to patch him up acceptable for a viewing.'

Tom pointed to another table on which a second body was lying covered in a shroud. 'That the sheriff?'

Doc Hawkins nodded and pulled back the shroud to reveal the alabaster-white face of the murdered lawman. He nodded his head with professional satisfaction. 'He's all embalmed and ready now, just waiting for Tod Gatlin to bring his coffin tomorrow.' He replaced the shroud. 'I'm afraid that it looks as if Pasco Springs is going to have a busy time with funerals.'

Rusty cursed, then: 'You said it, Doc. Especially if I get my hands on those murdering dogs!'

5

The Diamond T was a good fifteen minutes' ride from Pasco Springs. Tom let the roan have its head across the savannah, marvelling all the while at the lushness of Pasco Valley. And the experience of travelling across his very own ranch made him feel happy that he had put his trust in Lady Luck.

The ground rose to a little plateau beyond which rose the purple peaks of the Pintos Mountains. Then the ranch-house came into view, a single-storied affair solidly built of adobe bricks, with tall stone chimneys from whence streams of smoke drifted skywards. A broad, covered veranda paved with slabs of red rock stretched along the front of the house. A little over to the left were the corrals, barns and bunkhouse.

A lone young man with red hair was

sitting in a cane chair on the veranda, a bottle half empty beside him. As Tom approached and dismounted in front of him, he rose, melodramatically raising his glass and indicating a seat beside him.

'Ah, our new owner has come to inspect his property,' he said to the air, his voice slightly slurred. He lifted the bottle and pointed to a spare glass.

'Too early for me,' Tom said.

'But not for me,' said the younger man, draining his glass and replenishing it straight away. 'So we meet again, Mr Mallory!'

'The name is Tom. And I think we've met more than once. It was you that helped me out, I guess.'

'The least I could do after I grazed your horse. Sorry about that, but I was real peeved at you winning the Diamond T.' He shook his head as if to dismiss the thought and change the subject. 'And my name is Jeff. Jeff Trent, famous son of a once-respected citizen, now deceased thanks to the fine folk of Pasco Springs.' He drank half the glass. 'Rot them all, the bastards!'

'Jeff!' Nell Trent had stepped onto the veranda. 'Don't you think you've had quite enough of that stuff? It'll kill you if — '

'If the people of Pasco Springs don't do it first?' He looked defiantly at her then he bent his head, his face showing emotions that he clearly did not want to display. But Tom had seen them and recognized them for what they were. Jeff Trent clearly had feelings for his stepmother.

'I'll leave you to talk to Mrs Trent,' said Jeff, picking up the bottle and excusing himself.

Nell Trent apologized once he had gone. 'I don't know what to do with him, Mr Mallory. Ever since . . . ' Tears welled up in her eyes, but she fought them back. 'Ever since I lost my husband he's taken to drinking himself senseless. As you know only too well, that's how we've found ourselves in this situation.'

Tom grinned. 'You mean you and me

standing here on your veranda? All thanks to the whims of Lady Luck.'

Anger flashed momentarily in her eyes, but was instantly controlled. 'You mean your veranda, Mr Mallory. But yes, that's exactly what I mean. He seems bent on self-destruction.'

'Perhaps he's in so much pain he can't help himself, ma'am. Being around you all the time.'

Her eyes widened quizzically. 'What do you mean, Mr Mallory?'

'Jeff isn't much of a poker player, ma'am. He can't keep his emotions hid. That ain't exactly the look of a loving son he gave you. I'd say you have yourself an admirer.'

Nell Trent's cheeks flushed and for a moment she struggled for words. Then, controlling herself yet again: 'Come inside Mr Mallory, let me tell you about the Diamond T.'

'I'd be delighted,' he replied. 'Just one thing. Life will be easier if we get used to using the right handles. Mine is Tom.'

For the first time she smiled at him. 'Nell,' she said, before turning for the door.

Over coffee he told her about his meeting with Chester Harrington, when he had found out the size of the debt.

'How much?' Nell demanded.

'Twelve thousand dollars,' Tom replied. 'I saw it myself in Harrington's office at the bank. All signed and counter-signed.'

'Then he's a filthy thief and a liar,' she said. 'That's ten times what we owed. Jake was a good rancher, but wasn't much good at book-keeping. I took all that over from him. I know how much we owed, Tom.'

Tom rubbed his chin. 'Not too difficult for an extra zero to be added. That would explain a lot.'

Nell raised her eyes quizzically.

Tom went on. 'Harrington tried to pressurize me into selling the Diamond T straight away. He said I'd get enough to clear the debt and then some.'

Nell looked bemused. 'Then why on earth didn't you?'

Tom laughed. 'Cussedness, I guess. Besides, I'm curious as to why folk want the ranch so badly.'

There was a knock at the door then it was immediately thrown open. Two men shuffled in carrying the limp body of Jeff Trent between them. 'He's done it again, Nell,' said one, whom Tom recognized as the foreman who had defended Nell Trent in the Longbow the previous evening. 'He'll sleep until tomorrow, I reckon.'

'Put him into his bed, Jack, I'll keep a check on him.'

An hour later Tom and Jack Fisher were riding towards the eastern boundary of the ranch, so that Tom could begin to get a grasp of the lie of his land. It also gave him a chance to get to know his foreman and get his perspective on the history of the Diamond T.

'Been with the Diamond T long?' he ventured as they crossed grass and sage where small clusters of cattle were contentedly grazing.

'Twenty years and some,' Jack replied

taciturnly. 'You been a gambler long?'

The question revealed that Jack also wished to learn more about him. Clearly the foreman had already written him off as a tinhorn that had struck lucky.

'I've done a lot of things, Jack,' he volunteered. 'Not done much ranching, but maybe I know enough not to make a complete bitch of the job. Mostly though, I was a lawman.' And he recounted his reasons for turning in his badge and for turning to Lady Luck instead.

'I'm sorry to hear that, Tom,' Jack said after listening in silence. He offered his hand and the two men shook. 'I respect the law generally, Tom. I'm just sad that we don't have no real justice in these parts any more.'

'You talking about the lynching?'

Jack nodded. 'That and the fact that no one paid for the murder of Jake Trent. He was a good man, Tom. He wasn't no rapist. Me and the boys were all ready to go in and blast the town to kingdom come, but Nell stepped in. It wouldn't be what Jake would have wanted, she said. So for her sake we stayed our hand.'

'What about Jeff Trent?'

Jack clicked his teeth and shook his head in consternation. 'Can't figure him nowadays. Overcome with grief since his paw was killed, which is understandable. But his drinking! He'd already gone some ways to being drunk afore that. Started not long after Nell Trent came. Maybe he didn't like to see her replacing his maw.'

Tom pursed his lips. 'Don't take this the wrong way, Jack, but I hear tell that Nell was a mail-order bride. Any truth in that?'

Jack blew smoke from the side of his mouth. 'Maybe she was, Tom. Came out from somewheres back east and they were married before we knew it. Tell you one thing though, Jake Trent loved her fit to burst, just the way she loved him.'

'And how does Jeff Trent get on with

his stepmother?' Tom asked, watching keenly for the other's response.

'Respectful, I guess,' came the considered reply. 'Leastways when he's sober enough to get on with anyone. And that's been half the trouble lately.'

'How so?'

They crossed a shallow creek and entered terrain interspersed with thick tangles of sage and scrub. Some distance ahead they saw two Diamond T hands chasing and roping cattle. Beyond them smoke from a fire spiralled upwards.

'Well, Jeff always was a bit hotheaded. His paw was a good shot, but Jeff was something else. With a Winchester he could knock the warts off'n a toad at two hundred yards.'

'I've encountered his marksmanship before,' said Tom, pointing to the near-healed graze on the roan's rump.

Jack nodded sagely. 'Then that was a considered shot. If'n he'd meant to take your mount down, you'd a bin afoot quicker than you knowed it.'

'I guessed that,' Tom said, telling the foreman of his encounter with the bushwhackers as he climbed down into Pasco Valley.

'He's a good kid really,' Jake went on. 'But that headstrong streak could come out any time, especially when he's been drinking. We've been kinda wondering when all the pent-up anger over his paw will come out. And if it don't I'm fearful of letting him into town on his own. He could blow like a powder keg if'n someone applies heat to his fuse.'

They had reached the two hands, and smelled the smoke of the fire where a third hand was taking the roped young calves and branding them with the Diamond T.

For a few moments they watched as the three men worked as a team, two without leaving their saddles, the other on foot. One of the riders would chase a beast out of the scrub, then rope its head, drag it towards the fire so that it turned, while the other snared its pirouetting hind legs. Then the head roper, a lanky individual wearing a sombrero, whistled. Upon this signal his comrade, a short stocky bareheaded youngster backed up. In a moment the calf was stretched out, ready for the third hand, a cowhand with prodigious bow-legs, to leap forward to give the beast its hot tattoo.

'We're branding all the free calves,' Jack volunteered, as if divining the thought in Tom's head. 'Ordinarily we'd do them in the spring, but what with everything . . . ' His voice trailed off.

As another calf was released Jack introduced the hands to their new boss. Jack's friendly attitude towards Tom obviously meant a lot, for there was no hostility shown. Instead, they offered to let him give them a hand.

'You mean you want to see me make a fool of myself, huh?' Tom queried, taking a rope from Jack and heading into the scrub in search of a beast. However, after a couple of abortive attempts, and much resultant hilarity on the part of the hands, Jack shouted:

'Thought you said you'd had some ranching experience, Boss?'

Tom replied with a grin, 'I said some, but not how much.' And with that admission they good-naturedly took him under their wing. Leroy, for that was the name of the lanky sombrero-toter, demonstrated the technique of throwing the lariat. Flat loop, dipped loop, vertical loop, with amazing dexterity he snared calf after calf. And for each throw Leroy made, Clem, the shorter of the two ropers, demonstrated different types of heel loop for snaring the steer's hind legs. Finally, Jack demonstrated how to throw a hoolihan, a single flick rope ideally suited to rein in a full-grown Brahman.

Tom spent an hour gradually developing a passable skill with the boys as they saw that he was willing to get his hands dirty. Finally, Clem ventured an opinion. 'You just need practice to build up your arm muscles, Boss. Tossing cards ain't exactly the right training for roping steers.'

Tom joined in the joke. 'Laugh while you can, Clem. Give me time and I'll be roping you before you know it.'

'Yeah, Boss,' cried Leroy. 'You take his head and I'll snare his feet.' Grady chortled and held his iron aloft. 'And I'll be ready to brand his delicate pink rump.' And they again dissolved into good-humoured mirth.

'The boys are on your side, Tom,' Jack said later, as they resumed their tour of the range. 'To tell you the truth, I wasn't sure how they'd cotton to you.'

They were headed for the northern edge of the ranch, bounded by Pasco Butte in the foothills of the Pintos. The terrain had again turned from grass to sage, cactus and sand, through which a number of silver streams fringed with long grass babbled from the hills. They crested a hillock and saw below a crude timber building with a sod roof. Smoke oozed out of the single chimney, carrying with it the unmistakable aroma of coffee.

'A line shack out here?' Tom queried.

Jack nodded. 'That's right. This is

where Diamond T and Bar W land meets. And as you can see, we kinda get a giant helping of the water coming down from the mountains. Old Jake had this line-shack built twenty years ago, when there was more fear of Indians running off his cattle than there was trouble with greedy neighbours.'

'An' you still use it I see.'

Jack shook his head with a grin. 'We don't use it, Tom. That'll be Digger Brown, or one of his brothers in the prospecting fraternity. Jake used to let them have free ride across the land and free use of this old line-shack.'

At that moment the door of the shack opened and a grizzled, myopic old man dressed in clothes that looked as old as himself sidled out, an old Sharps poised at his shoulder.

'Digger, you old galoot, put that blamed cannon down afore you do yourself an injury!' cried Jack.

A wheezy laugh was followed by the Sharps being dropped from the worthy's shoulder as he hobbled out to meet them. Jack introduced the two men and the three chatted for a while until a paroxysm of coughing left the oldster a tad purple in the face. Tom looked concerned. 'You not feeling well, Digger?'

Digger tapped his chest. 'Just miner's lung, I reckon. Breathed too much rock and dust. Guess my lungs are probably full of more gold dust than I've ever dug up.' Another coughing bout was precipitated when he laughed at his joke, and when it subsided he produced a pipe and immediately lit up, producing clouds of thick, acrid smoke.

'Hey, maybe you should ease up on that hogshead you smoke,' suggested Jack. 'Your lungs can only take so much, Digger.'

The prospector guffawed as he dug in his vest pocket for a moment. Then he pulled out an ornate gold hunter watch. He puffed contentedly as he inspected it before mouthing a stream of invective that even Rusty would have been pleased with.

'I gotta be going, 'stead of jawing

with you two!' he exclaimed. 'I gotta see if'n that sawbones in Pasco Springs can brew up some decent medicine to settle this chest of mine. No point in being rich if'n you can't enjoy it.'

'Are you a gambling man, Digger?' Tom asked.

The prospector looked at Tom and feigned surprise. 'Why? You figure to win some of my hard-earned dough of'n me?'

Tom laughed. 'Me? Heck, I'm a simple rancher, Digger. No, I don't want to play you for any of your money. I just want to give you some advice, that's all. If you have come into wealth, I'd tend to stay away from the gaming tables. There's always someone ready to fleece a novice of the pot. Either that,' he added, 'or someone curious to know why a prospector suddenly gets an attack of good humour and takes to the cards. Just watch yourself is all I'm saying.'

Digger laughed his wheezy laugh again. 'Tom, you're looking at a man who's spent the better part of seventy years looking after hisself. What's that old saying about grannies and eggs.'

* * *

The Four Kings was an altogether different affair from the Longbow. It was bigger, brasher, and altogether more tasteless than Lucinda Grey's place. When Tom entered it that evening, he saw to his chagrin Digger Brown noisily ensconced in a card game, a half-empty bottle of whiskey by his elbow. Of the other players Tom only recognized the lanky pock-marked youngster who had been involved in the fracas with Jack Fisher the previous evening. His lip was swollen and when he grinned at Digger his missing tooth was apparent.

Digger saw Tom and melodramatically raised a finger to his lips.

The old galoot's doing exactly what I warned him not to do, Tom thought. He shrugged his shoulders and made his way to the bar, where Tyler Kent was standing, holding forth to a group of ready listeners.

Tom ordered a beer and was just raising it to his lips when a familiar voice growled sarcastically at him.

'Well lookie here, it's the pilgrim!'

Tom sipped his beer, then looked slowly round at Frank Wheeler. Behind him stood the leering Ben Jarvis.

Tom smiled, but without humour. 'I told you not to call me that again. Don't push your luck, Wheeler.'

'Don't push your luck, you mean. We don't like your kind around here. Trouble just seems to follow you — and people get themselves killed.'

'A sensible man would take that as a reason to step wary then.'

Wheeler stepped closer, his jaw muscles tightening belligerently. 'Maybe I'm going to run you outta town tomorrow, Pilgrim. Once I'm appointed sheriff.'

Tyler Kent suddenly detached himself from his group and turned with a grin. 'Ah Mallory,' he greeted. 'Come to savour the hospitality of my saloon?' He pointed to a handbill nailed to a nearby pillar. 'I overheard you talking to Frank here. As you can see, the town elders have decided to appoint a new sheriff tomorrow.' He clapped Frank Wheeler on the shoulder. 'We desperately need law back in Pasco Springs, don't we Frank?'

6

'It's a danged disgrace!' Rusty exclaimed as he brought the roan out of its box for Tom.

'What's a disgrace, you old muleskinner? I would have thought that you'd be pleased that your town is going to appoint a new sheriff.'

Rusty cursed. 'It's a disgrace that we're having a Wheeler set up as sheriff.'

Tom glanced at the discarded handbill that Rusty had balled up and thrown into the corner of his livery. He picked it up and smoothed it out, noticing that the election was to take place at ten o'clock that morning. He had gone to the livery to collect his mount prior to heading off to the Diamond T, and had not expected the old liveryman to be so incensed at the handbill's information.

'You could stand yourself, Rusty,'

Tom suggested, careful to keep any mocking intonation out of his voice.

'Pah! We need a lawman, not the bullyboy puppet of the biggest landowner in these parts!' He produced a brush from the voluminous pocket of his apron and started grooming the roan. 'You were a lawman, Tom. Why don't you apply?'

Slowly, Tom lit and puffed alight a cheroot. 'I used to be a lawman, Rusty. Then Lady Luck sent me a message that I should turn into a ranching man. And when you've finished and saddled my horse that's just what I'm going to do. Be a ranching man. Why, I've even learned to rope — a little.'

Despite his obvious annoyance Rusty groomed the roan gently. 'Ain't nothing to say you can't be both a lawman and a rancher. Why don't you toss for it?' He stopped grooming and held out the brush challengingly. 'Bristles up and you apply for the job. Wood handle and you drift off and be a pot-bellied rancher like Sam Wheeler.'

Tom chewed the end of his cheroot, conscious of the shrewd twinkle in the old liveryman's eye.

'Come on Tom, you know things ain't right round here. Lynching, bushwhackings and murder! You've seen at least two of them things.'

Tom blew out smoke and looked at Rusty through narrowed eyes. 'I'm intending to sort things out my own way,' he said.

'Pah! Best to do it with the backing of the law! Besides,' he added slyly, 'there are folks around here could do with the strong arm of the law. Mentioning no lady's name, you understand!'

Despite himself, Tom laughed. He had to admit that Rusty's logic was flawless. 'Damn you, Rusty! Go ahead and toss!'

Inevitably, it was an entirely male committee and electorate that had assembled in the Four Kings at ten o'clock. The committee, or town elders, consisted of half a dozen prominent business and professional townsfolk, namely Chester Harrington, Doctor William Hawkins, Tyler Kent, Sam Wheeler of the Bar W, Elmer Ludvigsen the local seed merchant, and Wes Lake the town telegraph operator. The saloon was full to capacity, most people partaking of free beer, courtesy of the Four Kings owner, Tyler Kent.

The six committee men were sitting behind three tables that had been slung together. They were conferring as Frank Wheeler ostentatiously strode in and walked up to the bar. Tyler Kent stood and banged the bottom of a bottle on the table, in lieu of a gavel, successfully bringing a hush to the room. 'Gentlemen of Pasco Springs, we have serious business before us this morning. We have a sheriff to appoint, and . . . ' he pointed to the gaudy gilded clock behind the bar, 'it's time to get started. I declare this public meeting open.' He gestured towards Chester Harrington, then sat down.

The banker rose painfully to his feet,

tugged his beard nervously, then read from some notes he had prepared. 'By authority of the committee of the town elders,' he smiled wanly at the audience who stood or sat sipping beer and smoking, 'that's us at the table, duly acknowledged by the men of Pasco Springs — that's you — we are here to agree upon the appointment of a sheriff, to take over the post vacated by Sheriff Dan Milburn.'

'Vacated when he was ventilated!' came an ungracious voice from the crowd. And typical of a southwestern saloon gathering, there was a smattering of laughter and ribald murmurings.

Sam Wheeler immediately shouted them down. 'That ain't funny! This is serious business. Dan Milburn was one of us and I want to remind you that he was murdered while serving in office.'

Silence reigned again. He eyed the whole crowd defiantly, then continued. 'A town and the surrounding territory needs law. Let's be sure and elect the right man.'

Chester Harrington nodded gratefully at the rancher. 'So everyone's seen the handbills advertising the post?'

A rumble of assent went round the room.

'It's a tough job, make no mistake,' he said.

'A damned well-paid job!' came a voice from the crowd, a different voice from the first, but one of the same ilk as the first heckler.

Chester Harrington held up his hand. 'Yes it is a well-paid job — as it should be. And we have only one applicant, Frank Wheeler over there by the bar. In my opinion he's — '

'He ain't the only applicant,' barked out Rusty, as he and Tom entered the saloon. 'I guess you've got a contest here.'

There was a chorus of laughter from a pocket of the audience.

'You planning to be the law, Rusty?' the first wit cried.

'That I ain't, but I guess I could do it a whole lot better'n a lot of you wasters,' Rusty countered, to another chorus of good-humoured approval.

Tom walked over to the front of the committee. 'Actually, I'm putting my name forward, gents. The name's Mallory. Tom Mallory.'

'The hell you are!' growled Frank Wheeler. 'We ain't having any damned drifter applying for a town job like this.'

'That's right,' said Sam Wheeler. 'You ain't eligible, Mallory. You're not from round here.'

Doctor Hawkins smiled. 'I think Sam may have a point, Tom. You've only been in town a day or two.'

To his right, a short man with a yellow moustache stood up. He was dressed in a collarless shirt with rolled-up sleeves. In his hand he held a ledger which he had been studying throughout. He stopped chewing on a wad of tobacco and pushed it into his cheek, where it bulged giving him a curious lopsided look. Tom recognized him as Elmer Ludvigsen the local seed merchant. He cleared his throat. 'A point of order is needed,' he began in a slow, ponderous delivery of speech. 'The town constitution says that for the sheriff's post the applicant only needs to be resident in the locality. There is no mention of any length of residency.'

'Staying in a cat-house don't count as residency,' cried Frank Wheeler triumphantly.

Tom smiled, yet with neither warmth nor humour. 'I'll pass on that remark — for now! But as for residency, I'm reckoning that being a local landowner round here would count.'

Ludvigsen nodded. 'Yes. Landowning will be doing.'

'I own the Diamond T,' Tom said to the assembly. 'I guess that gives me as much right as any of the Wheeler family to apply for the job.'

Sam Wheeler's jaw muscles tensed momentarily, while his nephew positively glowered at Tom.

The sixth member of the committee had been leaning back in his chair. He now sat forward and stood up. He wore wire-framed spectacles and had a pencil stuck from habit behind his right ear. This, together with his green shirt-protectors proclaimed his job as the town telegraph operator.

'I suggest we get on, gents. Time is money, so the sooner we get done and dusted, the sooner I can go transmit and receive the messages that make you gents as rich as Croesus.'

He sat down to a chorus of hollow laughter, which betokened the fact that a goodly number of the assembly were laughing without knowing what in thunder they were laughing about.

Wes Lake, the telegraphist, a man who knew more about comings and goings than anybody else in Pasco Springs, hoped that the same hollow laughter would make them realize the importance of what they were voting about.

Tom and Frank sat down at either end of the bar and fielded a barrage of questions put to them by the members of the town committee. Both had given an account of their past experience upholding the law. Tom had revealed his former existence as a constable in Dodsville, Texas. Frank Wheeler volunteered the locally known information that from time to time he had been deputized by Dan Milburn and his predecessor. His unofficial trouble-shooting at the Four Kings was also well known.

Then came questions about how they would deal with such situations as a mad dog on the loose; a bank hold-up; a crowd of rowdy cowpokes. The audience listened, at times heckling humorously, murmuring approval or disagreement. Throughout it all Chester Harrington acted as chairman, summing up each point, concluding that each candidate had answered reasonably.

At length, when the fund of questions seemed to have dried up, Tyler Kent laughed. 'Looks like we're going to have a shooting contest here, to decide on our new sheriff.'

'Suits me,' said Frank Wheeler with a grin that belied his words. 'How about last man standing?'

Chester Harrington coughed nervously and tugged at his beard, obviously concerned not to let the meeting get out of hand. 'We already know that both candidates know which end of a gun is which, so I think we can dispense with any — er — contest. I suggest, therefore, that the committee take a few minutes to decide.'

Tyler Kent stood and signalled to the bartender. 'A round of refreshments on the house!'

While the tide of humanity surged towards the bar, Rusty joined Tom. Tom asked: 'Is this how things are always decided in Pasco Springs? A public meeting, but with only six people allowed to vote?'

The liveryman nodded. 'Allus. Except that there's usually seven of 'em. The Padre sometimes throws his hat in the ring, but he's away visiting a sick relative this past week or so.'

'Are they elected representatives, Rusty?'

Rusty grunted. 'In a way, I guess they are. They're self-elected.'

A few moments later the committee reappeared from Tyler Kent's office.

'We've got a Mexican stand-off here,' announced Chester Harrington. 'Three votes for each man.'

'Then send for the Padre!' cried the slurred voice of a wit.

'Appoint 'em both!' shouted another.

Chester Harrington smiled thinly. 'I can't see a way round this. I think we may have to wait for the Padre's casting vote. Whenever he returns.'

Tom Mallory stood up. 'There is another way, gents.'

Sam Wheeler sneered. 'Cut cards again? I don't think so, Mallory. This is too important a decision to gamble on getting it wrong.'

Tom smiled. 'I wasn't talking about gambling. From what I hear the committee has been self-appointed, not elected.'

Chester Harrington blushed visibly and he fidgeted with his beard as he tried to find the words for a reply.

The reply came only too clearly from the floor: 'Yeah! We want to vote.'

'Let us decide for ourselves.'

'Who says you run things!'

The six committee members were exhibiting a range of emotions, from shock and amazement to outright anger. Sam Wheeler was the most vociferous. 'You'll meddle once too often, Mallory. If I was you . . .'

Doctor Hawkins put a gentle hand on the rancher's arm, then stood up, waving his hands for hush. 'Gentlemen, Pasco Springs is a small town and traditionally public issues have been decided by the committee. But we have to move with the times. The future is coming and perhaps Mr Mallory is right, maybe we should change the way we do things. Perhaps this committee should be elected. Maybe even one day we should have a mayor.'

A chorus of whoops of agreement met his words.

'I think we have the flavour of your feelings,' the doctor went on. 'But for a start, let's decide on which of these two candidates should be our new sheriff. We could take a straight vote on it, or we could ask some more questions?'

Rusty took a pace forward. 'I've got a question for them.'

Doc Hawkins indicated for him to ask away.

'How would you deal with a riled up rot-in-hell lynch mob?'

Doc Hawkins raised his eyebrows, then nodded. 'That seems a fair question.' He turned to Frank Wheeler. 'How would you handle it, Frank?'

The Bar W foreman glanced fleetingly at his uncle, then: 'If'n I was the sheriff I'd know danged well if the *hombre* was guilty or not. If he was innocent then I'd get Wes Lake the telegraph operator to send a message to the military, but if things got too hot in the meanwhile, I guess I'd take a few kneecaps off!'

He waited expectantly for a round of laughter to subside then continued. 'If he was guilty I reckon I'd know the mood of the town. Maybe I'd make myself a little less available.' He sat back smugly, expecting more laughter, which did not come.

'Huh! Can't say I think much of that!' came a lone voice from the far side of the room.

Tom looked through the crowd to see Digger Brown, the old prospector inspecting his hunter watch.

Doctor Hawkins turned to Tom. 'And how about you, Tom? How would you handle the situation?'

Tom stood. 'Well, as the sheriff my task would be to represent the law, not to make it. A man is innocent until proved guilty. And that means he would be my responsibility until a judge and jury made their decision.'

A murmur of approval ran round the saloon.

'If a mob decided to take the law into its own hands I guess I'd use a mixture of tact, diplomacy and a parcel of good deputies.'

The murmur grew into a general rumble of agreement.

'I'd make sure that I knew who I could call on at short notice. Men who share a pride in the town and who would uphold the law fairly and alongside me.'

Digger Brown stood up with a glass of beer in his knobbly fist. He raised it in salutation. 'Give him the job!' he cried. 'I sure as hell don't want some overexcited sheriff going shooting off folks' kneecaps.'

And with that the rumble of agreement turned into a tide of applause and enthusiasm.

Ten minutes later Sam Wheeler stomped out of the saloon with his nephew and entourage. Tom Mallory was already wearing the star given to him by Chester Harrington. But as he had pinned it on, the banker had taken the opportunity to remind him that his new appointment had no bearing on his debt to the bank, which was still outstanding.

Walking outside and crossing the street towards the Longbow, Tom playfully punched Rusty's arm. 'You've got a lot to answer for, Rusty!'

The liveryman laughed. 'Maybe! But I reckon you've got a couple of women you're gonna have to answer to first.'

Tom nodded. He was not at all sure how Lucinda and Nell would take to his news — for different reasons.

' 'Course, if'n it helps any,' went on Rusty, 'you can always make me your deputy if you need to make yourself scarce from some woman that's after your scalp!'

* * *

Digger spent a convivial afternoon soaking in a hot tub in the back room of the barber's shop, then he visited the doctor before stocking up on coffee, food and tobacco. Then, with his *burro* fed and watered he prepared himself to leave for his last week's work. He snorted as the town doctor's words came back to him.

'You've got consumption, Digger. You need to take it easy and let me treat you properly.'

Huh, he means he wants me to buy his expensive medicine, he thought. Well maybe I will when I come back a rich man.

He rode out of town in good spirits, oblivious to the fact that his every move was being watched.

* * *

That evening a small group of men sat in a room drinking whiskey. It was windowless and dark save for a single sputtering candle. 'This morning was a fiasco!' hissed a voice from the far side of the plane table.

The banker swallowed hard. 'I know. Frank should have been appointed.'

'Darned right I should!'

'Shut up!' hissed the voice. 'You screwed yourself up with that fool answer about lynch mobs.'

Another voice, with an amused, malicious edge to it broke in. 'So are we going to get rid of this sheriff too, Boss?'

'Not yet. I want the Diamond T and if things go the way I intend that they should, he's going to give it to me.' He laughed softly. 'Besides, if we give him enough rope, he may just hang himself.'

7

Chester Harrington was in his office an hour before Joe Watkins, his chief teller, was due to open up the bank. He had barely slept, despite the laudanum and the whiskey he had consumed upon his return from his clandestine meeting. The truth was that he was scared half to death. Scared of the men he had gotten involved with, scared of being found out for the things he had done and scared in case his nerves wouldn't hold out over what he was planning.

He puffed another cigar into life from the stub of the one he had just smoked, his third since he had let himself in. He sat back, tugging his beard as he allowed the cool, rich smoke to curl slowly from between his lips.

Smoke! Fire! It would solve all his problems. He smiled as he thought of his plan. His way to free himself from the grip of the others. And they had given him the idea when they had tried to set fire to the Longbow, when they tried to kill Mallory. It was a perfect plan. He'd torch his own bank, fake his own death and escape with more money than he'd ever need. More importantly, he'd escape from them! Escape from the risk of exposure as an embezzler of his own bank. He looked at his watch and with a sigh spurred himself into activity. He cleared his desk of all evidence of his research and preparation, then resealed everything in the large safe.

Yes, he reflected, it would be tricky when it came to it, but he'd manage. He'd choose the right time, when the town was at its most vulnerable. He puffed smugly as he thought of his own cleverness in fooling them all. He'd teach them for thinking that he could be pushed around. Manipulated like a puppet! And the blame would all fall on the man he intended to murder, whose body would be charred unrecognizably in the burnt-out ashes of the bank. Everyone would feel sorry for Chester Harrington, who had tried to save their money, yet got shot in the face for his pains.

He was interrupted from his reverie by the sound of Joe Watkins' keys in the lock. The chief teller was surprised to find his boss smoking and working in his office. 'Morning Joe,' Harrington replied to the chief teller's breezy morning greeting.

It would be easy, he told himself. All he had to do was get him to work late on some pretext when the day came. He smiled at Joe as he moved industriously about, getting things ready for the start of the day's business. It was quite amazing, he thought. If it wasn't for the beard and the limp, the two of them could just about pass for brothers. Yes, it would all work out well, Chester Harrington mused.

* * *

The sun was rising in a cobalt-blue sky as Sheriff Tom Mallory rode the roan towards the Diamond T. He wondered whether Nell Trent would take the news of his appointment any better than Lucinda had.

'Tom Mallory, you're a damned fool. Are you trying to get yourself killed?' she had remonstrated.

He had explained that Rusty had persuaded him that the town needed law.

'So you tossed for it!' she exclaimed, as he recounted how he had been helped to make his decision. 'Tom, one day you're going to run out of luck.'

He had silenced her with his lips and they had returned to her brass-framed bed.

He was grinning at the memory as he passed an outcrop of rocks big enough to hide a couple of concords, when a lasso dropped neatly over his shoulders. In a trice the loop was yanked tight and he was dragged backwards off his horse. He hit the ground hard, his breath exploding painfully from his lungs.

As he struggled to a sitting posture he saw three men, all wearing hoods and duster coats advancing towards him. One of them was coiling the rope that still ensnared him.

'What now, boys?' he asked, displaying a nonchalance that he did not feel. His heart was racing and his brain was searching for some way of improving his situation. His only hope at that point, he reckoned, was to keep them talking. Or rather, keep them listening, because they stopped and stood staring at him through their eye-slit hoods.

'Aiming to bump me off? Looks like being a habit round here, bushwhackin' sheriffs.'

Still no reply.

'Met you all before, I guess. Course you already know that. First time was when you murdered Sheriff Dan Milburn. Then when you tried to flush me out of the Longbow. And now you plan to finish the job, huh?'

The silence as they watched him was

uncomfortable to say the least. Tom reckoned that they must be enjoying themselves under their hoods. And that thought really angered him, but he knew that was the last thing he could afford to display. Apart from fear, of course. 'How much is the boss paying you boys?'

No answer.

'Must be a lot considering you're all going to hang when the law gets you.'

One of the figures at the back sniggered, an ugly noise that betrayed a lack of maturity. It brought a sharp turn of the head and an unspoken command for silence from the leader, the man holding the rope.

'Thought so,' Tom continued. 'At least that's what you've been promised, I guess.' He gave a short sarcastic laugh. 'Maybe you boys oughta play more poker, that'd teach you not to be so gullible, so willing to believe that there's such a thing as honour among thieves. Can you trust the boss?' Tom persisted. 'He's sent you on a killing spree already and the only thing you can be sure of is that he won't risk his neck. No sir, the hired help are always expendable at the end of the day.'

Maybe he'd hit home. He certainly seemed to have riled them up, because they exchanged glances and head-nods, then moved on him.

'Don't you think it'd be polite to take off those hoods?' Tom suggested. 'Or is that a stupid question to ask of cowardly curs?'

They were close to him now. The one with the rope was the nearest.

Tom suddenly fell sidewards, scissoring his legs as he did so to sweep the man's legs from under him. As he hoped, the lariat seemed to loosen a tad. He scrambled to his knees and strained his arms against the rope. If he could just get his arms free . . .

But it was too late.

A second man was on him, pinioning his arms beside him. And that was time for the third to calmly bring the butt of his gun down on the back of Tom's head.

There was the darkness of complete unconsciousness for some indeterminate time, then Tom felt as if he was swimming in a swirl of black nausea.

From somewhere he heard gunfire, and as he came to consciousness he realized his danger, his imminent death.

Struggling to open his eyes before the impact of a bullet snuffed out his life forever, he heard more shots and felt momentarily relieved that none of them had torn into his body.

And in among the shots he heard the sound of galloping hoofs.

He blinked in the glare of the morning sun and raised himself up on his elbows in time to see three rapidly retreating horses. Another shot followed them, then he turned and saw and heard the approach of a buggy.

'My God, Tom,' cried Doc Hawkins, laying his rifle aside and drawing to a halt. 'Those men were about to — '

Tom had managed to free himself

from the rope and had struggled to his feet. He put a hand to a pain at the back of his head, to find a trickle of blood. 'Going to kill me, I guess. Looks like I owe you my life, Doc.'

The doctor waved a hand in dismissal. 'I think I scared them off, Tom. The truth is, I couldn't hit the side of a barn, but my old gun makes plenty of noise. I keep it in the buggy to scare off rattlers and other reptiles when I'm on my rounds.'

Tom winced as the doctor examined his head wound. 'Well, I'm sure glad you saw off those snakes,' Tom said.

Doc Hawkins was absorbed professionally with Tom's head wound. 'It's just a small contusion and abrasion,' he mused. 'It'll heal all right without stitching.'

And without further ado he began examining the new sheriff for rib fractures. 'Always have to make sure that a cracked rib isn't misplaced,' he explained. 'A jagged rib can puncture a lung, which can kill you. Same thing goes for a torn blood vessel that makes you bleed into your chest.'

'Like Sheriff Milburn?' Tom asked.

Satisfied that there were no other injuries to speak of, the doctor nodded his head. 'That's right, Tom. I don't want to lose two sheriffs with internal bleeding. Folks might lose faith in my medical skills and start visiting Rusty instead.'

Tom laughed. Rusty had already told him of his little sideline in bottling and selling bosh water tonic, made from his iron-rich water-quenching trough.

'You headed for your new ranch?'

Tom nodded and tapped his star. 'I have to explain about my new appointment. And what about you, Doc? What lucky happening brought you out here in time to save my neck?'

Doc Hawkins laughed. 'Babies. Twins actually. I delivered them four days ago to a homesteading family, and they've got yellow jaundice. Probably nothing wrong, but with young twins you have to be careful. Maggie the mother is a natural maw, but her husband is kinda nervy.'

'Doctoring round here makes for a busy life, I reckon,' said Tom.

The doctor shrugged. 'On call every hour of every day.' He indicated the distant valley walls. 'I have patients spread out over fifty square miles. I do rounds three times a week. That's a lot of dust I swallow in that buggy there.'

Tom produced two cheroots from his vest and offered the doctor one, which he declined. He replaced one then struck a flame to the other.

'Why do you think those men wanted to kill you, Tom? Could it be personal or is it just because you're the sheriff?'

Tom let a trail of smoke drift from his lips. 'Two of them were the bushwhackers that did for Dan Milburn, I'm sure. The third I don't know for sure. My guess is that they're trying to keep the area free from the law.'

Doc Hawkins reached into his buggy and opened his little medical bag. 'I've got something here that I think I ought to share with you, Tom. I've felt kind of guilty that I've never told anyone about it, but until you were appointed sheriff there was nothing I could do with it.'

He drew out a small packet and opened it to reveal a tuft of red hair.

'I got this from Betsy-May Elmore's dead hand, when her body was brought to me for embalming. Maybe you'd best take it off my hands, then my conscience is clear.'

Tom looked at it for a few moments. 'I hear that Jake Trent, the murdered man was a redhead. This his hair, Doc?'

Doc Hawkins looked back, his expression non-committal. 'That's just it, Tom. All I can say is that it could be. Which means that it might not.' Then he looked awkward, embarrassed even. 'But until this very moment I've had no one to share this with.'

* * *

Tom found himself talking to the roan as he rode towards the Diamond T. He had parted company with the doctor, who had headed east to visit another homesteader whose broken leg he had set the day before.

'If this tuft of red hair was really Jake Trent's, then it looks pretty damning. But if it wasn't his, then it could have been his son Frank's. And that puts a whole different complexion on things, doesn't it?'

The roan's ears twitched, almost as if it had understood what he was talking about.

'Certainly could explain some things,' he went on. 'Lust? I've seen men go plumb loco with lust. And I've seen the way he looks at Nell Trent, his step-mother. Could he have been aiming at removing his father to get Nell?'

The roan's ears twitched again.

'I know,' said Tom. 'That could explain the drinking. Could be trying to blot out guilt.'

The ranch-house came in sight and the roan whinnied as another rider came out to meet him.

It was Nell Trent herself. Her eyes opened wide when she saw the star on his chest. Her bottom jaw fell open, but no sound came out.

'Surprised, huh?' he said, divining the meaning of her expression. 'Yeah, thought I ought to ride out and let you know that I'm the new sheriff round here.'

She shook her head in exasperation. 'Nothing you do will surprise me, Tom. I was expecting you yesterday and was starting to get worried. I thought maybe — '

'That maybe I wasn't coming back? That I might have sold out?' He shook his head with a grin. 'But if those three jaspers that I ran into on the way here had their way I guess I'd be buzzard-meat right now.'

And he explained all about the events that had happened since he had last seen the Diamond T. 'So if Doc Hawkins hadn't come along, I wouldn't have been here at all.'

They dismounted in front of the

ranch-house and went in. Tom smoked a cheroot while Nell made coffee.

'But why, Tom?' she asked as she came with a tray bearing a steaming coffee pot, cups and a plate of freshly baked cookies.

'Why become sheriff, you mean.' He shrugged. 'Because it seemed the right thing to do at the time.'

'Yet you still owe the bank a lot of money — not as much as they say — but if they foreclose on you, you'll lose everything.'

Tom sipped his coffee. 'True, but that's one reason why I let Rusty talk me into applying for the job. If I'm the law, there's no way I'm going to let the bank or Chester Harrington cheat their way to ten thousand dollars — or the Diamond T.'

Nell looked worried. 'So those men who ambushed you today, were they the same ones who bushwhacked Sheriff Milburn?'

'Can't be any doubt, Nell. Except there were three of them today.'

'And you think they could have something to do with the Diamond T? With someone wanting it, I mean.'

Tom stubbed out his cheroot. 'All routes seem to lead to the ranch, Nell.' He stood and put a hand on her shoulder. 'I'm sorry to say, but I think your husband's — er — murder, was also one of those routes.'

Nell stared up at him for a moment, then stamped her foot as tears welled up in her eyes. 'Damn their plan. And damn this ranch. Jake was a good man. Why, Tom? Why?'

Tom shook his head. 'I don't know, Nell. But I'm going to find out.'

A creaking floorboard and a heavy tread at the door was followed by Jeff Trent's appearance. As usual he had a half-empty glass in his hand.

'Find out what — Boss?' he asked sarcastically.

Tom eyed the younger man distastefully. 'For one thing, why you seem so set on drinking yourself to death.'

Jeff Trent drew himself up to his full

height and advanced lumberingly into the centre of the room. 'That — is my business!' he said slowly, enunciating every word defiantly.

'Jeff, please control yourself,' Nell pleaded.

'That's right, mister,' said Tom. 'Otherwise someone's going to take control of you once and for all.'

In answer Jeff nodded and bowed melodramatically. 'In that case, sir, I'd best watch myself when you're around.'

'Just watch yourself, mister,' Tom said quietly. And picking up his hat he turned to Nell. 'I'm afraid that I'm going to have to ask you to look after the ranch more than I anticipated.'

Jeff squinted at Tom, seeing the star for the first time. 'So . . . o . . . o! Our boss is now also our local sheriff! Seems you're planning to take over everything round here?'

Tom turned towards the door. 'Like I said, Jeff, you just watch yourself.'

Nell followed him out and watched

him mount the roan. 'Tom, I understand what you're saying about looking after the ranch. There's something going on in this valley and I'll help all that I can, but just tell me — what was all that about with Jeff? You seemed cold to him. Why?'

Tom pursed his lips as he thought about the tuft of red hair that he had inside his vest pocket. He decided to say nothing about it to Nell at this stage. Instead he said: 'I'm concerned about you, Nell. How safe is Jeff to have around?'

The woman coloured as she looked shocked. 'Jeff is no problem to me. He drinks too much, I know, but he's still grieving over his father's death. When that grieving is over he'll stop drinking. I know it.'

Tom nodded non-committally. 'I hope you're right, Nell. Meanwhile just watch him and look after yourself.'

* * *

Tom was just riding out of the ranch when Clem came galloping towards him. The youngster's eyes widened when he saw the star on his chest. 'Jack sent me to get you, Boss. We found Digger Brown up by the old line-shack. He's dead. Some bastard backshot him and cleaned him out.'

8

With Jack Fisher's help Tom brought Digger Brown back to town in a buckboard. Doc Hawkins shook his head sadly as he took charge of the body.

'He was a dying man,' he said. 'His lungs were near played out. I told him he had to be careful, but I certainly didn't expect him to die of lead poisoning like this.'

Tom woke the following morning to the touch of Lucinda's lips on the back of his head. For some moments in hurt, which surprised him, until he remembered why.

'You poor sweet, this lump is almost as big as a hen's egg. You were lucky whoever hit you didn't break your skull.'

Tom turned and grinned up at her. 'Lady Luck's my mistress, remember, honey? And I guess I'm luckier than poor old Digger Brown.'

Lucinda sighed and tears began to well up in the corners of her eyes and form droplets on her black eyelashes.

'Lucinda, what's wrong? I'm OK!'

She sniffed and wiped the tears away with the back of her wrist. 'I know, Tom. It's just that you seem to live life so fast. Either we're making love here, or you're off having folk try to kill you.'

He gave a short laugh in an attempt to make light of it. 'You said yourself that excitement should be my middle name.'

'I know I did, Tom. And I like excitement. But hell, we've only known each other a few days and there's just been so much of it.' She kissed his forehead and then left the bed to draw on a silk dressing robe and pull back the lace curtains.

Tom watched her move about the room, all too aware of what she did to him. In only a short time she had come to mean so much. And that worried him. He rolled out of bed and dressed quickly.

'I've had enough of Pasco Springs, Tom,' she said at last, looking down at the street below, where people were already going about their business.

He came up behind her, encircled her waist and rested his chin on her shoulder. 'Funny, I think this place has a lot to offer. You, for instance.'

'And your new job, Sheriff Mallory!'

He spun her round and stood looking down into her still tear-stained eyes. He wiped a tear trail from her cheek. 'What's brought this on, Lucinda? We're having fun, aren't we?'

She averted her eyes. 'Fun, Tom? Yes it's been terrific. I just don't want it all to end with you dead in some alley or bushwhacked out on the range somewhere.'

'That isn't going to happen, Lucinda. I've got a hand to play in whatever game's going on here. And it's a hand I mean to win.'

'Is it always a game for you, Tom?'

He lifted up her chin and kissed her gently. Then he said, earnestly, 'Life's a game, Lucinda. I believe that, but my absolute rule is to play every hand seriously.'

'Does that include me, Tom?'

He kissed her again. 'Especially you, Lucinda. I'm as serious as I've ever been in my life.'

She grabbed both of his arms. 'Then let's grab our chance, Tom. Let's just leave Pasco Springs behind us. I'm scared of this place now. I've got money and so have you. You could sell the Diamond T as soon as you want and we could go anywhere we want.'

He shook his head. 'I can't, Lucinda. Not yet. I've taken on responsibilities here.'

She broke free and made for her adjoining bathroom. 'That's what I thought you'd say,' she said wistfully.

He watched her close the door after her and he cursed himself silently. In truth, he was aware of seething emotions inside himself. He hadn't intended for anyone ever to get as close to him as Lucinda had. He couldn't bear re-experiencing the pain he had suffered when Annabelle had been killed. Maybe it would be better if I just left now, he thought. Walk away before one of us gets real hurt. He looked out of the window at the street below. He watched three riders cantering down the dirt street, dismount then stride into the Four Kings, outside which the barkeeper was sweeping the boardwalk.

One of them interested him in particular. A tall lanky one with a limp. A shiver ran up his spine, as if hackles were rising.

When a smiling Lucinda returned a few moments later, with her spirits uplifted from a good womanly weep and a refreshing wash, she found that Tom had gone.

* * *

Tom pushed open the batwing doors of the Four Kings, allowed his vision to accommodate to the dimness of the interior, then stepped inside.

It was deserted except for three men standing at the bar helping themselves to coffee from a large pot left on the counter. They had turned upon hearing Tom's footstep.

'Well what do you know,' said Frank Wheeler, sarcastically. 'The new sheriff with his new badge. Come to throw your weight around?'

Tom pointed to the coffee pot. 'Shouldn't you boys be paying for that?'

Ben Jarvis sneered. 'We don't pay. We're special guests of Tyler Kent.'

'You mean you're paid help,' returned Tom, still eyeballing Frank Wheeler and ignoring Jarvis, much to the latter's displeasure.

'You gonna take his lip, Frank,' said the tall, lanky, pock-marked youth, with a whining voice.

Tom kept his eyes on Frank Wheeler. 'Well, Wheeler, are you paid help or aren't you?'

A muscle twitched on Frank Wheeler's jowl and his brow furrowed. 'I work for the Bar W,' he replied. 'We're just friends of Tyler Kent and enjoy his free hospitality whenever we're in town.'

'Yeah, special friends,' Jarvis reiterated.

'And we sometimes do our friend special favours,' chirped in the sallow youth.

Frank Wheeler stiffened slightly. He barked at the youth: 'Shut it, Zach!'

Like a child receiving an unexpected castigation, the youth slumped back against the bar and fumbled in his vest pocket. He drew out an ornate gold hunter watch and began fiddling with the winder.

Tom recognized it immediately, and he fancied that he saw Frank Wheeler flash a look of warning at the youth.

'What's your name, boy?' Tom asked.

The youth pocketed the watch and, looking at Frank Wheeler received a tilt of the head that indicated that he should reply. 'Fargo. Zach Fargo, if it's any business of yours.' His eyes narrowed. 'And I ain't no boy,' he added defiantly.

Tom had turned full on to him now, a smile playing across his lips. 'Oh it's my business all right, Zach. I'm the sheriff of Pasco Springs, you see. And that means I've got the right to ask suspects any questions I see fit.'

Jarvis stood erect. 'Suspects? Suspects of what, mister?'

'Murder!' Tom replied. 'You see, that watch you're carrying doesn't belong to you, does it Zach? You stole it off Digger Brown after you backshot him.'

Frank Wheeler took a pace forward. 'Now hold on, Mallory. You've no proof that watch ain't Zach's own, given to him by his grand-pappy.'

A nervous smile trembled across Zach Fargo's mouth. 'Yeah, it's my grand-pappy's watch.'

Tom nodded. 'That could be the truth,' he said. 'But it's as likely as saying that the moon gets a chunk eaten by a dragon every night. Besides, I'm also intrigued to know how come Zach here got his limp.'

The youth's eyes widened anxiously. 'You calling me a liar? As for my leg, I fell off my horse day before yesterday and snagged it on a rock.'

The smile vanished from Tom's face. 'Not much of a poker player, are you boy. And the answer to your question is — yes, I am calling you a liar!'

Zach Fargo's brow was moist with sudden perspiration, yet he was young, vicious and riled. He pushed himself away from the bar to face the sheriff with an aggressive posture. He was sure that if it came to it he'd have the backing of his two companions.

But Tom Mallory simply held up his hand and stated calmly: 'No one makes a move here. Playing with guns is one sure way for someone to get hurt. And as for you, Zach Fargo, I have reason to believe that watch you're carrying is the stolen property of Digger Brown, a prospector that was backshot yesterday. If you've got a bullet graze on your leg

— which I'm supposing you caught a few nights ago after trying to bush-whack me, when Curly O'Toole got killed — well, I'll take a dim view of it all.'

Fargo went for his gun, but never got close. Before any of the trio knew it a Navy Colt had jumped into Tom's hand and there was a click as the hammer was thumbed back.

No one moved a muscle as the gun was raised and brought down hard to pistol-whip the kid. Then, as he slumped to the floor, Tom reached down and pulled back his trouser leg to reveal a bandanna crudely tied over an obvious bullet graze.

Tom holstered his weapon, tucked Zach Fargo's Peacemaker into his waistband, and then unceremoniously hauled the youngster to his feet.

'Don't anyone even think of interfering with the law!' Tom said, as he dragged the near senseless kid towards the door.

'Hey, what's going on here?' came

Tyler Kent's indignant voice as he emerged from his office.

'Just cleaning some vermin out of your saloon, Mr Kent,' Tom said, without slowing his walk. 'I'm arresting him for suspected murder.'

* * *

News of the arrest spread around Pasco Springs like wildfire. Opinion polarized almost immediately into those who were vocal in their support of Zach Fargo and those who were adamant in their decision to say nothing. The truth was that no one liked the pockmarked youth, yet because it was believed that he was one of the town's hard men, people felt it would be injurious to their business and their health to curry disfavour among his friends.

Rusty Reardon, however, was not one to worry about upsetting anyone. He called on Tom as soon as he heard. He glared at Zach Fargo through the bars of his cell. 'You young bastard!' he said through gritted teeth. 'If I had my way with you — '

'But you don't, Rusty,' said Tom. 'The law will decide. And that means a judge and jury. So, until the circuit judge gets here I'm going to keep the suspect in custody here.'

Zach Fargo sneered at them. 'You won't be holding me for long. I've got powerful friends in powerful places. When they hear about this, and when they feel the time is right, they'll get me out.'

Rusty made a lunge through the bars, but Fargo stepped back, his face creased with an ugly leer. 'When I do get out of here I'm going to settle with you, old man. And you, Mallory! I ain't forgetting that thump on the head.'

Tom felt the bump on the back of his own head and smiled. 'Nor did I,' he replied before turning away from the temporarily dumbstruck youth.

Tom put a hand on Rusty's shoulder and urged him to sit on one of the plain wooden seats. 'The law will see to him,

Rusty,' he repeated gently.

Rusty let out a string of invective, then: 'You need help, Tom. You can't look after the young — suspect, all the time. You need a deputy.'

He puffed his chest out and despite himself Tom laughed. 'You old galoot, you talked me into this job and now you're talking me into deputizing you. You sure you don't just want this star?'

Rusty scowled. 'Dang it, Tom. I just want to see the law do the right thing by Curly and Digger. If this young bastard had anything to do with it, I want to be part of the law process.

'Besides,' he added with a hint of a grin. 'Mrs Grey wouldn't be too happy if'n you're spending all of your time over here in the jailhouse.'

Tom shook his head good-humouredly and opened a drawer in his desk. He drew out a deputy's badge. 'As a matter of fact, Rusty, I had the very same thought in mind and had this all ready. Now raise that dirty paw of yours while I swear you in.'

* * *

It was a busy day after that. First Tom paid a visit to Wes Lake in the telegraph office. The little man's eyes twinkled behind his wire-framed spectacles when Tom entered the office.

'Been expecting you, Tom. Need to send a special, eh?'

Tom grinned. 'Circuit judge needs to be notified. Wouldn't happen to have a notion where I can get hold of him, would you Wes.'

Wes Lake beamed smugly. 'I know exactly where Judge Tulloch is, Tom. I took the precaution of finding out as soon as I heard about young Fargo's arrest.' He shoved a telegram sheet and a pencil towards Tom. 'Just write down what you want to say and I'll have it off faster than you can say 'Circuit Judge'.'

As Tom wrote, Wes drummed his stubby fingers on the desk. 'You figure he did it, Tom?'

Without looking up Tom replied: 'If I was a gambling man I'd be willing to bet a pile.' Then he looked up and smiled as he handed the message to the telegraphist. 'But seeing as I'm a mere officer of the law, I'd say it's up to Judge Tulloch and a jury.'

They chatted for a few moments until Wes pointed through the window at the limping figure of Chester Harrington coming up the street.

'Banker's day to send his weekly message to his backers,' he explained, self-importantly. Tom said nothing, but bid Wes good day. He tipped his hat to Chester Harrington as they passed, his gambler's instinct telling him that some part of the banker's message would relate to his own precarious debt over the Diamond T.

His next visit was to the seed merchant Elmer Ludvigsen, who seemed to Tom a solid enough character.

'This is a dangerous business, this arrest,' Elmer volunteered. 'This young ruffian has friends and he works for Sam Wheeler. You could find yourself in a tight corner.'

Tom nodded. 'That's why I'm seeing who the law can call on, Elmer.'

The seed merchant chewed tobacco reflectively and nodded. He clenched his fists, so that his forearm muscles bulged. 'In my younger days I could pack a punch, Tom. Yes, and if needs be I can fire a gun too. I am ready if you need.'

They shook hands and Tom went on his way, visiting a variety of tradesfolk across the town. Darkness was falling by the time he was back in his office. He found his new deputy drinking coffee and talking ten to the dozen to Zach Fargo, who was lying on his cot with a pillow round his head. Tom laughed. 'Rusty, do you reckon you can hold the fort for a while longer? Lucinda and I have kinda got some unfinished business to take care of.'

Rusty patted the Peacemaker he had strapped to his waist. 'Take all the time you want, Tom. Me and Fargo here are having a swell time. I'm telling him about the days when we hanged dirt like him just for showing themselves to decent folk.'

Fargo rolled over on the cot, pretending to be asleep.

* * *

'Tom, I wanted to tell you something this morning before you ran off to arrest that hoodlum,' Lucinda said. 'I'm not Annabelle.'

He looked at her hands, then at her beautiful dark eyes. 'I know that, Lucinda. And I . . . '

From somewhere outside there came the report of a single gunshot.

In a trice Tom was on his way out. People were milling about unsure whether to seek cover or investigate the source of the gunshot.

'Anyone see anything?' Tom shouted. There was a chorus of negative replies. Then he saw that the door of his office was wide open. With his gun out he crossed the street, edging his way towards the open door. Then he saw

Rusty slumped back in his chair, an enlarging circle of blood covering his chest. His head hung down, his chin resting on his blood-soaked shirt.

'My God, Rusty!' cried Tom, quickly ensuring that there was no one else in the office before holstering his weapon. Through the bars of the cell he saw Zach Fargo lying sprawled across his cot, the whole of his face a bloody, gaping hole.

'Tom . . . ' Rusty gasped. 'Get Doc — '

'Easy, old-timer,' Tom whispered, looking round for someone to come to his aid. A couple of men appeared at the entrance and Tom signalled them in. 'Look after him for a few moments,' he ordered.

Rusty groaned and grabbed his wrist, his face contorted with pain. 'Get Doc.'

Then his eyes glazed over and his head lolled to the side as a death rattle escaped from his lips.

* * *

Three men sat drinking by the light of a single candle.

'Now it's time to close down the Diamond T,' said the one with the bottle.

9

The Reverend Phineas Ambler was a tall stick of a man with red veins covering his cheeks and nose, a consequence it was widely rumoured of him having imbibed well in the fleshpots of the West before he had seen the light and been called to God. Even so, two days after the killing of Rusty Reardon and Zach Fargo, he found himself with five funerals to conduct on that same day. Virtually the whole town had packed into the small clapboard church and listened while he sermonized over the five coffins.

All in all he did a good job of it, reflected Tom as he watched the padre working the mourners into a display of emotions, unusual in the south-west, where folks kept their feelings mainly to themselves. Yet as he watched the townspeople as they filed out, he could sense the disquiet and anxiety that was unspoken. It hung like a tangible cloud. Five men were dead, and no one was behind bars. Tom was aware of the inevitable glances in his direction, as much as if to ask what he was doing about it.

Tom ushered the padre aside afterwards and engaged him in conversation about the killings. Then he asked: 'Where is Jake Trent buried?'

The padre looked shocked. 'A murderer and a rapist! You won't find him buried in the hallowed ground of my cemetery.'

'So where was he buried?'

'His wife and son took his body back and buried it somewhere on the Diamond T. I don't know any more. I was never asked to perform a service. They must have just planted him — and what does that tell you, Sheriff, huh?'

Tells me a whole lot about you, thought Tom. He pointed his hat at the crosses in the cemetery. 'A lot of youngish men seem to have died these last few years.'

The padre rubbed his lips with the back of his hand. 'Meaning what, Sheriff?'

'Not sure, Reverend,' Tom replied. 'But I guess I'd like to have a look at your church register.'

* * *

As he rode towards the Diamond T, Tom went over the recent events in his mind. And as he did so he found his temper rising at whoever was behind things in the valley. His ire was not improved upon arriving at the Diamond T to find Jeff Trent in a full-blown drunken stupor. He was sprawled on a cane chair on the veranda, an empty bottle by his side.

Nell Trent and Jack Fisher came across the yard to meet him as he tied the roan up to the hitching post. 'How long has he been like it this time?' Tom asked.

'Since last night,' Nell replied, with concern written across her face. 'But it's just one bottle after another and if I say anything to him it just makes him worse.'

Jack nodded in agreement. 'I dunno what we can do about him, Boss. He's gonna kill himself unless he sorts himself out.'

Jeff Trent's eyelids flickered open to reveal bloodshot, bleary eyes. 'Someone talking about me?' he slurred. Then he lapsed back into semi-stupor.

Tom turned to Nell with his jaw set firm. 'Enough is enough, Nell. He needs curing and fast. I've a few things I want to get straight with him. I'd appreciate it if'n you could make a heap of black coffee.'

Nell nodded without a word, clearly relieved to be trying anything to help him. When she had gone inside Tom turned to Jack. 'And if you'll help me carry him, we'll begin his cure now.'

Between them they half dragged and half carried Jeff Trent across the yard.

Jack looked doubtfully at Tom, as their destination became all too apparent. 'You meaning to drown him, Boss?'

'Nope,' replied Tom, as they arrived at the horse trough. 'Just sober him up.' And so saying, he propelled Jeff fully clothed into the cool water. In he went, struggled for a moment, then burst from the water gasping for air. Tom let him take in a few breaths, then ducked him again. Three times he repeated the process, and each time Jeff cursed and struggled harder. Then he struck a blow at Tom, a real haymaker had it connected. But Tom dodged it effortlessly and as quick as lightning delivered a firm slap on each cheek, then pushed him back into the water.

'I'm . . . gonna . . . kill you!' Jeff threatened once he had struggled to a sitting position. Noticeably, his voice sounded determined and had lost some of its slur.

Tom grinned, but without humour. 'Well, you can try, right after you drink a barrel of coffee that your stepmom is busy brewing.' He signalled Jack and together they hauled him out of the trough and frogmarched him back up to the house.

It took the better part of an hour, a couple of jugs of coffee, a vomiting session, then a couple of jugs of water, but at last Jeff Trent could have been considered more sober than he had been in many days.

'And you're going to stay sober, Jeff,' Tom commanded.

A sneer began to form on the young man's lips. 'Says who? You ain't my keeper.'

Tom nodded. 'But I am your boss, whether you like it or not. It's time you stopped acting like a spoiled brat. You've given your stepmom enough grief already.'

Jeff looked at Nell and two blotches of red formed on his cheeks. 'Don't call Nell my stepmom. I'm almost the same age.'

Nell looked confused and helpless. 'Jeff, please . . . '

But Tom held up a hand. 'Don't worry Nell, Jeff and I are going to sort out a few things today.'

'The hell we are!' Jeff said defiantly. 'I'm going to bed after all of your roughing me up. And as for Jack Fisher, I'll — '

'You'll do nothing,' Tom interrupted. 'And I'm not arguing with you, Jeff. I'm telling you as sheriff of Pasco Springs that you're going to help me. I'm investigating a whole passel of murders and I want you to start acting like a man instead of something that crawled out of a bottle. You're going to show me your paw's grave.'

Nell took a sharp intake of breath and covered her face with her hands. Then recovering: 'I'll come too, if you want?'

Tom shook his head. 'No! I mean I need Jeff to show me on his own. And then I need him to ride somewhere with me.'

Jeff Trent stared at him for a moment, then he slowly got to his feet, his eyes looking moist. 'OK, Sheriff.

Give me five minutes to change, then we'll go see my paw.'

It took them twenty minutes to reach the small hillock which overlooked a babbling stream that fell into a pool, around which several of the Diamond T herd of Brahmans were wading in to lap up the cool water.

There were a couple of willows atop the hillock, and two graves.

They had ridden in near silence, which Jeff now broke. 'I buried him here with maw.'

They had dismounted and now stood with hats in hands, paying their silent respects.

'He was a good man, Tom,' said Jeff, his eyes now completely welled up with tears. 'He didn't deserve what they did to him.'

Tom asked. 'Are you truly sure he was innocent?'

Jeff's bent head turned sharply, his eyes flashing sudden anger. 'Course I'm sure! Paw was a good man. He was framed.'

'Who by, Jeff? Who would have a motive?' And he watched the younger man for any signs of guilt. Any suggestion that he could be lying.

Jeff shook his head. 'It beats me. I've agonized about it for ages. I just can't get anywhere, though. It all just hurts, hurts like hell.' He turned and looked Tom square in the eye. 'That's why I drink, Tom. It just hurts so much.'

Tom said nothing about the tuft of hair in the envelope in his pocket. Instead, he asked: 'Why didn't you do anything about it if you think your paw was murdered? I guess a lot of men would have wanted to torch the whole town, get anyone who could have been involved in that lynching.'

Jeff licked his lips, as if feeling the need of a strong drink. 'Because of — her. I can't explain it properly.'

Tom looked puzzled. 'I'm not sure I understand, Jeff. I've seen the way that you handle a gun and I reckon if you let loose you could do a whole lot of damage, but you didn't.'

'No, I've numbed my brain with drink.'

'Because you don't think your stepmother would want you to go seeking revenge?'

Red blotches formed on his cheeks again. He bent his head, then: 'Damn it, it's because if I went on the rampage I'd surely end up dead. That's why I drink. At least being a useless drunk I still get to stay around her . . . '

Tom nodded understandingly. It confirmed what he had thought all along. 'You're in love with her, aren't you Jeff?'

Jeff didn't look up or say anything, but the sobbing that racked his shoulders told all.

* * *

Tom smoked a cheroot as they rode towards the northern boundary of the Diamond T, to where it abutted the Bar W as both ranches' land ran into the mountains.

'It doesn't make sense, Jeff,' said Tom. 'Why would Zach Fargo kill Digger Brown? Surely not just for a watch. OK, so he was bragging about striking it rich in town, but all miners do that. The question is, did he really? And if he had, does someone know about it and want to move in on his claim?'

Jeff clicked his tongue thoughtfully. 'It sure sounds like it, Tom. So what do we do now?'

Tom pointed up ahead, to where the trail began snaking up into the mountains. 'Do you know where Digger was working?'

'I know where he pitched his camp. He had a sodroofed affair up thereaways.'

Tom nodded. 'Then let's go see.'

They had just started to move on again when a group of horsemen broke cover from a cluster of scrub oaks up ahead. They strung out in a line across the trail, blocking the way ahead. There were five of them. In the middle was

Sam Wheeler riding a tall grey and he was flanked by his nephew, Frank Wheeler, and Ben Jarvis. A couple of Bar W hands flanked them.

Sam Wheeler raised himself in his saddle and called out: 'Hope you don't think you're going across Bar W land, Mallory? Especially not with that Trent trash!'

Tom sensed Jeff's stiffening beside him and stayed him with a raised hand.

'I'm going up that trail, Mr Wheeler, whether its Bar W land or not. And if you interfere with me, then I may have to arrest you and your boys there for interfering with the due process of the law.'

Jarvis grunted some remark to Frank Wheeler, who guffawed and muttered something to his uncle. Sam Wheeler's eyes narrowed. 'You may not be sheriff much longer, Mallory. Can't say I'm impressed with the way you've been doing your job. Just how many men have been killed since you were appointed?'

'I'm going to get the men responsible, Mr Wheeler,' Tom returned. His gaze shifted directly on Ben Jarvis. 'You mark my words.'

Sam Wheeler sneered. 'Better be quick then. I've got more than I can handle just trying to keep my boys from riding into Pasco Springs to deal out their own justice. They don't like the fact that their friend, Zach Fargo, got murdered in your jailhouse.'

Jeff bristled. 'And what're they gonna do? Go in and lynch another innocent man?'

Sam Wheeler studiously ignored Jeff. 'Let's cut to the chase, Mallory. You've got the Diamond T and I want it. I'm still willing to pay good coin for it. Why don't you just sell up and high-tail it out of Pasco Valley for good?'

Tom grinned. 'And leave this lovely ranch and my brand new job all at once?' Then the grin vanished. 'Why, you would think that people have got an unseemly interest in the Diamond T.'

Frank Wheeler spat contemptuously on the ground. 'Uncle Sam, I never did see what you saw to be so good about the Diamond T. It's just scrub-land with inbred cattle and a whole load of vermin that look after them.'

Jeff seethed. 'You calling my boys vermin, Wheeler?'

Frank Wheeler laughed maliciously. 'Trent, I'm saying your hands are next to useless and your family don't amount to a pile of horse-shit.'

Jarvis slapped his knee. 'Except her, Frank. Except that calico princess old man Trent bought and paid for.' He grinned defiantly at Jeff.

Tom guessed what was happening. The goading was working. Jeff was rising to the bait. He put out a restraining hand towards his young companion.

'Guess I wouldn't mind paying her myself,' Jarvis went on gloatingly.

Jeff's hand had shot towards his iron. 'Then you can pay the devil!' he cried, his gun clearing leather.

Jarvis's eyes had opened wide and a grin had begun to form when he saw Jeff's starting movement, and he too went for his gun. But the explosive crack of Jeff's gun and the thud of a bullet in his chest wiped the expression from his face as he was lifted backwards to tumble dead in the dust.

A fraction of a second after Jeff's shot, another gun fired and Jeff Trent slumped forward in his saddle, an ugly streak of blood spurting from the left side of his abdomen.

'Drop the gun, Wheeler!' cried Tom, both Navy Colts out and covering Frank Wheeler and the other two hands who had both got hands on guns, but as yet had not drawn.

Frank Wheeler simply grinned and nonchalantly replaced his gun in its holster. He raised his hands to chest height. 'No need for that, Mallory,' he almost crooned. 'Your man there drew and killed my friend. I shot to protect my uncle from that madman.'

Tom had dismounted and holstered

one of his own weapons, keeping them covered with the other, while he inspected Jeff's wound. After a cursory examination he was relieved to see that it was a non-fatal, though ugly abdominal wound. Jeff was in pain and looked as if he would pass out any minute.

'We all saw it, Mallory,' grunted Sam Wheeler, his voice quavering slightly from shock. He nodded to his two hands, who dismounted to check on the obviously dead Ben Jarvis.

'That man's a murdering dog, just like his paw,' he said upon the confirmation of Jarvis's demise. 'You've got a duty to arrest him and take him into custody.'

Tom glared at the rancher and his grinning nephew. 'I know my duty,' he said, trying to keep the raw anger out of his voice.

'Sure you do, Sheriff,' beamed Frank Wheeler. 'But can I suggest that you take the prisoner back to Pasco Springs real soon, afore he dies of blood loss.

We don't want to cheat the noose of a murderer, do we?'

* * *

Doc Hawkins had rushed over to the jailhouse in answer to Tom's message.

'He's a lucky young man,' said the doctor after he'd treated the wound and bandaged Jeff up. 'An inch to the left and he would have had a perforated spleen that would have killed him in ten minutes.'

Tom rubbed his jaw. 'He's luckier than that Jarvis feller, Doc. But I wouldn't say his current position in a jail cell was especially enviable.'

Doc Hawkins washed his hands in the basin and dried them on a towel while Tom locked the cell. Already Jeff was asleep from the potion the physician had administered. 'I hope history isn't about to repeat itself, Tom.'

Mallory cringed, despite himself. 'Jeff Trent is going to get a fair trial,' he said emphatically. 'He was goaded into it, Doc.'

The door suddenly opened and a whirlwind that was Nell Trent burst in, followed by Jack Fisher. She eyed Tom distastefully, her eyes burning with emotion. 'How could you . . .?' she said accusingly. Then: 'How is he?'

Doc Hawkins looked awkwardly from one to the other. 'Jeff will be OK — that is, his wound will heal, Mrs Trent. I'll — er — keep an eye on him the next few days.' And picking up his hat and medical bag he excused himself and left.

'How the hell did this happen, Tom?' Jack demanded.

Tom explained exactly what had happened, apart from being economical with the truth about Jarvis's aspersions about Nell's character. Jack listened understandingly, while Nell stood looking through the bars at Jeff, as if not taking any of it in.

'So it was a fair shoot-out?' Jack asked.

Tom clicked his tongue. 'Except that

Jeff drew first and the other man is dead.'

'But you'll stand up for him?' Jack persisted.

'I'll try,' Tom replied. 'Trouble is, it could be my word against theirs. And there are two Wheelers and two of their hands who saw it happen.'

Nell suddenly spun round. 'Sam Wheeler! So he's going to get all that he wanted. First my husband, now my . . . my . . . ' Her eyes welled up with tears as she sought to find the right words. 'My Jeff! And then it'll be the Diamond T itself.' She gave a single great sob, then took a deep breath. 'But I'm not going to let that happen. I'm going back to the Diamond T — then I'm going to pay the fine Mr Sam Wheeler a visit!'

Before either Jack or Tom could do anything, she had stormed out of the office, mounted her horse and ridden off.

10

Tom was about to follow Nell when Chester Harrington stepped through the threshold of the still open door. 'My now, where is Mrs Trent off to in such a hurry?' he asked.

'Exactly what I'm planning to find out,' Tom replied. 'If you'll excuse me, Mr Harrington.'

But the banker showed no sign of wishing to excuse him. He stood his ground, pensively tugging his beard. 'I'm afraid that I have urgent business that I need to discuss with you, Sheriff. It's about your debt to the bank.'

Tom smiled thinly. 'I wondered when you'd be getting along to see me.'

The banker looked up at Tom. 'I have the interest of the bank to consider, Mr Mallory.' He produced a paper from inside his jacket. 'I'm afraid that I have to formally give you this document, since the bank is calling in your loan. We require full payment of the loan by close of business tomorrow evening — or you forfeit the Diamond T.'

Tom stared back po-faced. Then without changing his expression he took the document and tossed it contemptuously onto his desk. 'I'm thanking you, Mr Harrington, because now we have something on paper.'

The banker's eyes moved nervously and his lips moved but produced no sound.

'The thing is,' Tom went on, 'the loan seems out of proportion to the amount actually borrowed.'

'In . . . interest, Mr Mallory. Banks are entitled to interest on loans.'

Tom smiled. 'Legal interest, that's true.' Then the smile disappeared. 'But not interest that's suddenly increased by someone adding a zero at the end of a figure.'

The banker's cheeks went purple. 'Wh . . . what are you suggesting, Sheriff?'

The smile reappeared, only it was a smile devoid of warmth. 'I'm suggesting nothing, Harrington, except that maybe the law will be looking at the dealings of the bank before any more business is done.' He took hold of the little banker's arm and turning him round, escorted him onto the boardwalk. Then: 'Let's just say that once I've taken care of a few important issues I'll be coming to see you.'

And with a final smile he went back into the office and closed the door.

Jack Fisher was looking bemused. He looked even more bemused when Tom opened a drawer in his desk and produced a deputy's badge. 'Raise your right paw, Jack,' he ordered, as he pinned the badge on his foreman's shirt. 'Don't have much time, so I'm deputizing you to look after Jeff, until I get back.'

'You're going after Nell, aren't you?'

Tom was already half out the door. 'I've got to make sure she's not going to run into danger. We've got enough trouble as it is.'

* * *

Sam Wheeler sat in the deep leather armchair in his office surrounded by a cloud of smoke, which emanated from a charred old pipe. Since his return to the Bar W he had smoked furiously and downed several glasses of his best whiskey. Altogether a hard man by anyone's estimation, as witnessed by his success in building up the Bar W over three decades, yet the events of the day had badly shaken him.

'Thank God you're a fast man with a gun, Frank,' he said to the other man sitting on the other armchair by the window. He raised his glass.

It was the umpteenth time he had done so. And it was the umpteenth time they had drained their glasses. 'Pity about poor old Ben,' Frank said, hanging his head, as if deeply upset.

Sam helped himself to another glass. 'Yes, I'm sorry about that, Frank. I know he was a good friend of yours.

But at least that Trent trash will hang for his murder.'

Frank looked at his uncle, inwardly laughing at the way the old man was slurring his words. 'Then I guess you'll get the Diamond T like you planned.'

'Exactly so my boy.' He beamed at his nephew with genuine affection. 'And one day you're going to be the richest man around here. When I've gone this'll all be yours.'

Frank Wheeler grinned as he looked around the study with its bookcases, Indian wall-hangings and ornaments made out of carved longhorns. At the desk, old maps and faded paintings of frontier scenes. It summed Sam Wheeler up, all the trappings of a self-made rancher. Old things of the past, worthless stuff! Just like the old man himself, he thought malevolently.

Sam Wheeler suddenly stood up and crossed to the window. 'Now who in tarnation is that?'

They both looked out of the big window and watched as a cloud of dust told them that a rider was fast approaching the ranch-house. 'Why it's the Trent woman!' Sam exclaimed.

Behind him Frank Wheeler's face broke into a grin.

* * *

Nell Trent had intended to ride back to the Diamond T and get a gun. But as she had ridden furiously out of Pasco Springs with the wind rushing past her face, she literally cooled down. You stupid girl! she chided herself. What would a gun be any use for? She was angry, furious with Sam Wheeler, but she had no intention of killing him. No, I'm going to tongue-lash him, she told herself. It might not do much good, but at least it will make me feel better, she decided.

So instead of heading for the Diamond T she rode around for a while to clear her head, then she headed for the Bar W. To her surprise nobody was around. Nobody had intercepted her on the road into the enclosed yard in front of the sprawling ranch-house. She dismounted and tethered her horse to one of the wrought-iron hitching posts, each of which was topped by a Bar W branding iron.

The place seemed eerily deserted. Then she saw the ranch-house door standing ajar. For the first time she felt hesitant, less sure of her intended course of action. But she steeled herself, reminding herself that Jeff was lying sedated in the Pasco Springs jail-house, because of Sam Wheeler and his machinations to get control of the Diamond T. She called out: 'Sam Wheeler, it's Nell Trent! I want to talk to you!'

No answer. So, she pushed open the door and entered the spacious hall. It was paved with large marble slabs in the Mexican hacienda style. Her boots clicked on the floor, announcing her entry. 'Sam Wheeler, I said I want to talk to you,' she called, crossing the hall to another open door, the first of a row of three. She looked round the door into a large spartanly furnished sitting room, which was empty.

She called out again as she looked round the next door. It was a study that smelled of strong tobacco. Again she was about to turn away when she saw a pair of boots lying behind the desk.

Whether out of curiosity or suspicion she did not know, but she walked into the room and looked round the back of the desk. The she gasped as she saw Sam Wheeler lying on his side.

'Mr Wheeler, my God!' she said, going to him and dropping to her knees to half turn him towards her. His head rolled and his unseeing eyes stared up at her, immobile and lifeless like the eyes of a child's doll.

She raised her hand to her mouth to stifle a scream, but when she saw, then felt the hot sticky blood on her hands she let out a real scream, which she quickly suppressed. In moving the body a pool of blood spread across the floor, like a dam opening to release a flow of water. Then she saw the knife protruding from the old man's side. And the numerous bloodstained slashes told her that it was only the last of several fatal wounds. Looking at it sticking in his body seemed somehow obscene to her. She grasped the handle to pull it out.

It was then that she heard the click of a gun hammer being drawn back, followed by a voice grating menacingly: 'Don't move a muscle, lady!'

* * *

Tom had urged the roan to cover the ground as fast as it could, in the belief that he would catch sight of Nell. But when he reined to a stop outside the big barn at the Diamond T and was informed by Clem and Leroy that Nell hadn't been back, he cursed himself for being seven kinds of a fool. Quickly he told them to drop whatever they were doing, and for Leroy to accompany him, while Clem rounded up the rest of the crew and went to meet Jack Fisher in Pasco Springs.

'Where're we headed, Boss?' Leroy asked.

'The Bar W,' Tom replied. 'And let's just hope that Nell's guardian angel is awake today.'

They rode like the wind itself and were rewarded when they caught sight of Nell's dust trail in the distance. They saw her dismount in the Bar W yard, then disappear into the ranch house. A full two minutes later they were dismounting themselves and rushing into the Bar W ranch house.

Across the hall they heard a man's raised voice, cursing and hurling aspersions at someone. They virtually skidded into the room together, and saw the aged Bar W cook holding a gun outstretched, covering a kneeling Nell Trent. Her hands were covered in blood and on the floor in front of her lay Sam Wheeler's body, with a large knife sticking out of his side.

A Navy Colt appeared in Tom's hand

and he barked an order at the cook: 'Drop the gun, mister, if you want to keep on breathing!'

Then they heard the cocking of a gun behind them, followed by Frank Wheeler's voice.

'No, you drop your weapon, Mallory! Sheriff or no, you've got no right to be ordering folk around on our ranch.'

Tom cursed silently, then very deliberately reholstered his weapon.

'Mister Frank, Thank God!' gasped the cook. 'I found her, sir. Look! She's green-rivered the boss!'

On hearing this Frank Wheeler pushed past Tom. 'What's that you say, Skeeter? Then spying his uncle's body he ran forward, his eyes wild with alarm. 'Uncle Sam!' His head slowly revolved to look down at the cowering and sobbing Nell. 'You damned Trents!' he bellowed. 'You goddam murdering Trents!' He raised his free hand, balling it into a fist, as if intending to strike Nell.

Tom's hand went to his gun. 'Steady

Wheeler!' he grated.

Frank Wheeler froze for a moment, as he seemed to struggle to compose himself. Then he re-holstered his gun and spun round to face Tom. Tears filled his eyes and his voice cracked with emotion. 'Get her out of here, Sheriff. You've got a witness to this. Now take the murdering bitch and lock her up.'

* * *

The Pasco Springs jailhouse had never seen the like on two counts. First, no one could recollect a woman ever being held prisoner. And second, it was the first time that a cell had curtains over its window and a French dressing screen across one corner to allow changing and ablutions in some sort of privacy. Both of these had been installed on Lucinda Grey's insistence.

Tom had not slept all night as his mind went over and over the events of the day. It was as if the world had gone mad. Within a few short hours Jeff Trent and his stepmother had both killed, and he had no choice but to lock them up until they stood trial.

Jeff had been drifting in and out of consciousness and Doc Hawkins feared that the wound might be infected, causing both a high fever and a state of delirium. Certainly his reaction upon seeing Nell being shown into the adjoining cell was less than rational.

'Nell, my sweet, dear Nell,' he had mumbled. 'So you've come to your senses at last!'

It had taken a long time for Nell to say anything. Almost as if her mind had switched off to prevent her from focusing on the awful events. Finally, once in the cell, and with Lucinda by her, she had recounted her steps from leaving the office with violence in her mind, until she had found Sam Wheeler dead with a knife in his side.

'It wasn't me, Tom,' she had said, her eyes full of the horror of it all. 'He had already been murdered!'

Her words rang through Tom's mind as he and Jack sat smoking in the office with mugs of coffee in their hands. 'This is one hell of a mess, Tom,' Jack said. 'You know that neither Jeff nor Nell are killers, don't you?'

'Of course I know it, Jack. The evidence though, is pretty damning. The Bar W cook was perfectly clear about finding her with the knife in her hand.'

Jack snorted in disgust and dropped his quirly into the stove, having lost his taste for the tobacco. 'It was that blasted nephew of his, Tom! You know it and I know it. Now why don't we go and beat the truth outta him?'

Tom took a final puff of his cheroot then deposited the butt in the open door of the stove. 'We're not going to do that for two reasons, Jack. First, it's against the law. And second, he's got almost the whole town behind him. The name of Trent has probably reached an all-time low. Besides, Sam Wheeler's money has kept a lot of people around here in business.'

The day wore on and Tom left the office, now heavily guarded and surrounded by Jack and the Diamond T crew. Leroy and Clem positioned themselves on the boardwalk on either side of the sheriff's office, while Grady and two of the other boys took turns in watching the back door and the back alleys. Tom virtually repeated his earlier round of the town, calling on the likes of Wes Lake and Elmer Ludvigsen, to see just how many of the townsfolk he could call upon at short notice. To his chagrin, he found that there were fewer than had previously expressed solidarity. For one reason or another the name of Wheeler had more weight than that of Trent.

The sun was going down when one of Lucinda's girls came over to the jailhouse with two baskets of food for the prisoners and Tom's men. She pointed through the window to the Four Kings down the street. Kerosene lamps had been lit and they could hear the rumble of loud voices.

'It gave me the creeps passing the place,' she told Lucinda. 'Tyler Kent is letting them have free drinks, and that Frank Wheeler is getting them all stirred up.'

Lucinda looked worriedly at Tom. 'Tyler's not a fool, Tom. He holds a lot of sway in this town.'

'I know, Lucinda,' Tom replied. 'And he's swaying them the way he wants.'

Lucinda scowled. 'Not if I can help it!' And without further ado she tossed down the serviette she had in her hand and made for the door. 'I'm going to get Tyler to see reason.' Tom and Jack watched helplessly as she picked up the hem of her dress and crossed the street, heading for the Four Kings.

'It . . . it's going to get ugly isn't it, Tom?' Nell said, standing behind the door of her cell, her hands gripping the bars so that her knuckles were white. She looked down at Jeff, tossing and turning deliriously on his cot in the next cell. Despite her fears and anxieties, she smiled at him.

Lucinda strode purposefully into the Four Kings, ignoring the variety of stares and comments that greeted her. The mood in the place was distinctly uncomfortable and hostile. Tyler Kent saw her and immediately detached himself from the group he had been drinking with and came to meet her. 'Lucinda, a pleasant but most unexpected pleasure seeing you here.'

'Can we talk, Tyler.'

He pointed to his office door at the rear of the saloon, then led the way through the crowd. As he opened the door and let her in he turned and nodded to Frank Wheeler.

Lucinda walked into the office then spun round to face the saloon owner. 'Tyler, what's happening?'

He shook his head innocently. 'Nothing. Just men letting their hair down.'

She squared up to him, her hands on her hips. 'That's not true. You're letting that mob have free whiskey. What are you planning? Another lynching?'

His eyes narrowed and an ugly leer spread across his face. 'Maybe the town wants justice.'

Lucinda shook her head. 'You're mad! We can't afford another lynching.'

His eyebrows rose demonically. 'Why only one?'

Lucinda stared back in disbelief. 'You can't mean it! Not a woman!'

The saloon owner shrugged. 'What does it matter what sex a murderer is?'

She had no time to react, to dodge the vicious uppercut that lifted her off the floor and slammed her unconscious across the desk. Tyler Kent leered as he rubbed his knuckles. Then he calmly turned and locked the door.

* * *

Chester Harrington had finalized his plans. He had ensured that Joe Watkins had enough work at the end of the day to keep him working into the night. He had told him that he'd be back later to help him. What he didn't tell him was that he'd be back with a Derringer in his pocket and a can of kerosene. He had his things ready and was about to let himself out of the door when he heard the rumble of the crowd, as it erupted from the doors of the Four Kings. He pulled the door open a crack, then almost fell back as it was forced open. 'Going somewhere, Chester?' Frank Wheeler asked, his face twisted cruelly.

'To . . . to the bank,' replied the little man, tremulously. 'I . . . important business.'

Frank Wheeler shook his head. 'The boss wants you with me at the party.' He grinned savagely and half dragged the little banker out into the street to join the front line of the noisy mob. A myriad of torches danced in the air above them.

'Welcome to the necktie party, Chester,' Frank Wheeler cried.

11

Peering through the window Jack said, 'Looks like they've stopped outside the Four Kings. They sure look like a swarm of bees that's mad as hell.'

Tom unlocked the weapon rack and started handing out rifles and extra ammunition. 'I guess they're waiting for someone to give them a lead.'

'There's folk coming over from some of the side streets,' Jack said. 'They look friendly.' And a few moments later a small group of people including Elmer Ludvigsen, Wes Lake and Doc Hawkins came knocking at the door. 'This I hoped never to see again,' said Elmer. 'Another mob. We've come to help.'

'Tom, what's going to happen?' Nell cried through the bars. Her voice quavered on the verge of hysteria. 'They're coming for Jeff and I, aren't they?'

Tom tried to sound confident. 'They're not going to get through that door, Nell. We've got a lot of fire-power here.' He turned to look out the window at the slowly advancing crowd with the torches bobbing up and down. He silently mouthed a curse then issued orders to the Diamond T boys to take their weapons and form a hard line outside on the board-walk.

Doc Hawkins caught Tom's elbow. 'Tom, I have a suggestion. As I see it, it's the only way out of this situation.' Tom gestured for him to outline his plan. 'It's risky, I admit,' said the doctor. 'You let me and Nell take Jeff out the back way to my place. If we can make it no one will think of looking for them there.'

There was no time for deep consideration. Tom nodded. 'Let's do it!'

* * *

Chester Harrington was feeling distinctly uncomfortable. All his plans were going wrong. And this wasn't supposed to happen. Frank Wheeler had marched him to the front of the mob, where he was horrified to find that he was being hailed as a sort of figurehead. A seal of approval to their intended actions.

But it was a lynch mob! No place for me, he thought. Again his hand closed on the Derringer in his pocket and he thought about making a run for it. But then cold reason told him that Frank Wheeler wasn't going to let him run anywhere, even if he could run with his limp. Just seeing the wild-eyed irrational faces told him that this crowd wanted to see blood spilt and lives taken. No, there was only one thing for him to do and that was to go with the crowd. Maybe he'd be able to slip away soon.

'Looks like the sheriff's got himself a team of deputies, Frank,' said a burly cowpoke beside them. 'Armed too.'

Frank Wheeler spat. 'They may be armed, but they're not going to shoot.'

'How d'you know, Frank?' cried someone close.

'Because this is town business. Besides, who's going to stand up to a small army like this?'

The same doubting voice replied. 'That sheriff knows how to shoot. You saw that, Frank, when he took Zach Fargo in.'

Frank Wheeler rounded on the man, his teeth bared. 'He draws fast, but you ain't seen him shoot, have you! Now shut up.' He turned to the crowd and raised his arms. 'Listen up all of you. In that jail there are two lousy murdering Trents. They're dogs and don't deserve to live. They killed my Uncle Sam and my best friend Ben Jarvis.'

To Chester Harrington's even greater displeasure and discomfort Frank Wheeler put an arm about his shoulders, directing attention to him. 'They're not only murdering scum, but they're robbers. They've been bleeding the bank dry. That's your money they stole — ain't that right, Chester?'

There were angry jeers and cries for Harrington to add his weight to the cause.

'Ain't that right, Chester?' Wheeler persisted, his hand now gripping the little banker's shoulder so hard that it made him squirm.

'Th . . . that's right. They're swindlers!' He gulped, for his mouth was parched with fear. 'They've swindled the bank and that means they've swindled all of you.'

Frank Wheeler grinned triumphantly. 'So what're we gonna do?' he cried.

'Get 'em!' was the unanimous cry.

* * *

The mob advanced to the sheriff's office and spread out across the street in front of the boardwalk.

'That's far enough!' cried Tom. 'You can see that my deputies and myself are all heavily armed.' He held up his shotgun to emphasize the point. 'So whatever you're all aiming to do, if you'll take my advice you'll forget it. One step nearer and I'll take that as an illegal act. And none of us here are in a bluffing mood!'

There were many grunts of discontent.

Frank Wheeler raised his arms above his head and the crowd quietened. 'Back off, Sheriff. This gathering is Pasco Springs itself.'

Wes Lake tapped his rifle. 'You don't speak for all of Pasco Springs, Frank Wheeler.'

This drew a smirk from Frank Wheeler. 'No, but I speak for them as believes in justice. And Pasco Springs has a way of dealing out its own type of justice.' He pointed at the line of deputies on either side of Tom. 'If you'll all take a piece of friendly advice, you'll make yourselves scarce and let justice be done.'

Tom didn't move a muscle. Nor did any of his companions. He gave a thin smile, then: 'You're not talking about justice and you know it. And so do the rest of you. Lynching is the action of evil, unthinking cowards.' He scanned them, his eyes falling on several members of the mob that he recognized. 'And lynching a woman is something no man could ever be proud of.'

'She green-rivered Sam Wheeler in cold blood,' cried a voice from the crowd.

'That hasn't been proved,' Tom returned. 'My prisoners haven't been found guilty of anything. Now I say disperse and go home before someone gets hurt!'

'Maybe you'll be the first to get hurt, Sheriff!' cried another anonymous voice from the mob.

'Could be,' Tom said. 'But this shotgun with a hair trigger says that a lot of you are gonna get peppered.'

There was a nervous mumbling, for there was not a man present who was unaware of the damage that a shotgun could inflict at such short range.

'Step aside, Mallory,' growled Wheeler.

'You know we've got right on our side.'

Tom pointed contemptuously at his opponent. 'Is this your leader?' he asked the mob. 'And was he the leader last time?'

Another wave of nervous muttering told Tom that he was right. That slight chink in the mob's solidarity might give him a chance, he thought. 'And who got you all so fired up, anyway? Most of you have been drinking all day, haven't you? And how much have you all spent?' He laughed sarcastically. 'I'm willing to bet that you've hardly parted with a cent. Zilch! It's all been free, hasn't it?'

Nobody argued. Nobody disagreed.

'All free thanks to Mister Tyler Kent, I'll bet.' He squinted theatrically and peered into the crowd. But where is Mister Tyler Kent? He's not here, is he?'

And heads started rapidly turning and twisting as everyone suspiciously began searching among themselves for the saloon owner.

'I ask you again,' said Tom, 'where could he be? And why is he letting you all do the dirty work?'

⋆ ⋆ ⋆

Lucinda's jaw hurt like hell and her head felt as if it had been hit with a sledgehammer when she came round. She tried to raise a hand to her lips, to wipe away the sticky copper-tasting blood that was oozing from her burst-open lip where her teeth had cut it, but she could not move.

Then she was aware of the heavy weight on top of her and the gloating face looking down at her. She was lying on the floor and Tyler Kent was astride her, kneeling on her arms.

'So you've come back to the land of the living, have you?'

Lucinda shook her head as if to help her eyes focus and her mind think. 'Let me go, Tyler!'

'Why? I've got you where I want you, Lucinda. On your back.'

She struggled, and was instantly rewarded with a swipe across the cheek with the back of his hand. 'You should have been nicer to me, Lucinda. I offered you everything once. But you turned me down, didn't you?' His face contorted into a mask of pure evil. 'Now I'm going to take what I want — for nothing!' Then his eyes rolled and he chuckled malevolently. 'Just like I did with little Betsy-May.'

Lucinda froze and stared up at him in horror. 'You raped Betsy-May?'

He nodded, drawing a knife from under his coat. He caressed her cheek with the point. 'Sure I did, before I killed her. Oh, not with a knife like this. I strangled her.' His eyes gleamed as he looked at the blade in his hand, and went on, almost conversationally: 'Good make of knife, this is. It's a sister to the ones that killed Rusty Reardon and Sam Wheeler. I sell them for a dollar in my emporium.'

'You're mad!' gasped Lucinda, struggling again.

Tyler Kent's eyes seemed to bulge out of his head and he leered evilly. 'As mad as a skunk!' he said, raising the knife above his head, ready to stab downwards.

* * *

'Don't listen to him!' cried Frank Wheeler. 'He's just trying to put us off our purpose.'

Tom shook his head. 'I'm just trying to understand why every man jack of you is willing to commit murder. And make no mistake about it, that's exactly what it would be. Cold-blooded murder — if you get past me, that is.'

'Step aside, I say,' demanded Frank Wheeler.

Again Tom and the deputies stood resolute. 'And just what is our respectable town banker doing here?'

The banker looked petrified, but said nothing.

'I'll tell you what he's doing here,' Tom went on. 'He's obeying orders.

That's right, isn't it, Harrington? You've been told to come.'

'I . . . I . . . ' stammered Chester Harrington.

But Tom continued. 'Your boss wants to control everything around here, including the Diamond T. And that's really what this is all about, isn't it? Get rid of the Trent family, get rid of me, then your boss gets his paws on the Diamond T.'

'Back off, Mallory,' grated Frank Wheeler.

The mob was growing restless and opinions were becoming fragmented. There were calls to get on with the job. Others called on Tom to explain what he meant. Still others were pressing to hear from Chester Harrington. Tom played to the mob. He shook his head sympathetically. 'Poor Chester Harrington! Kind of got caught in the middle, haven't you? Your boss put pressure on you to get the Diamond T, so you've cooked the books at the bank, haven't you?'

Harrington was sweating and visibly trembling. 'It . . . wasn't my idea . . . ' He looked helplessly at Frank Wheeler. 'Tell him, Frank — '

'Shut up, you lummox!' Wheeler growled.

But Chester Harrington's nerves were close to snapping point. He looked up pleadingly at Tom and his deputies. 'I didn't, I didn't mean . . . ' His voice trailed away as Frank Wheeler grabbed his arm.

'You leave him alone, Frank Wheeler!' cried Wes Lake. 'Let him talk.'

Chester Harrington looked gratefully at the telegraphist. Indeed, he seemed to gain some inner strength from Lake's intervention. He pulled his arm away from Wheeler and turned to Tom: 'I was made to do it. They made me — '

'I said shut up, or be shut up,' Wheeler growled.

The little banker's eyes turned on him, and emboldened by the feel of the Derringer in his pocket he realized how much he hated this jumped-up cow-poke. 'And that's the last time you'll threaten me, Wheeler!' His hand was out of his pocket, the Derringer starting to rise, when Frank Wheeler drew and fired at point-blank range. The .45 bored a hole in his chest and the little banker was thrown back against the wall of the mob.

Tom spun the shotgun onto Frank Wheeler, his finger on the trigger. But he knew that a shot would take out more than just Frank Wheeler. And in that moment of hesitation he lost the initiative. Frank Wheeler turned and pushed into the crowd, but not before his gun had barked, winging Wes Lake. Tom shucked the shotgun aside and hurriedly barged into the mob in pursuit of Wheeler.

* * *

Lucinda screamed as the knife descended. There was a thud as it was stabbed into the floorboard a couple of inches from her left ear. From somewhere outside came what sounded like a fusillade of gunfire.

'Sounds like the necktie party is starting up,' Tyler Kent said, his eyes smouldering with lust. 'Maybe your boyfriend is already dead.' He grinned as her expression mirrored the pain his remark had caused. 'Now you're going to get what you deserve!' he said, roughly grabbing the front of her dress and ripping it off her shoulder to expose her bosom.

'You bastard!' she cried, bucking with all her might. But it merely seemed to inflame him more and he reached down to undo his buttons.

It was a movement that gave Lucinda a chance, which she grabbed with gusto. She turned her head and sank her teeth into his supporting wrist, causing him to cry out and momentarily lose his balance and drop his guard. That moment was all she needed. With her free hand she wrenched the knife out of the floor and raked the blade across his exposed throat, showering herself with crimson blood. Wide-eyed he fell sideways and Lucinda immediately rolled away and jumped to her feet. With contempt she watched him writhe, his breath rattling grotesquely in his severed windpipe as he tried in vain to hold his bleeding throat closed. Then she kicked him in the groin. 'And that's for Betsy-May, you low-down bastard!'

As she towelled the blood off her as best she could, she heard the noise of the mob rising. Then out of the window, in the moonlight she saw Frank Wheeler run round the corner then dash up a back alley. A few moments later Tom followed, heading for the same alley.

Then several shots rang out.

12

Jeff lay on the couch in Doc Hawkins' consulting room, his face lathered in perspiration after the exertion of getting from the jail. He was only dimly aware of what was going on around him. Yet as he lay there gripping hard on Nell's hand he had a smile on his face that incongruously hinted at contentment.

From outside, seemingly from all over town came the noise of shouts, breaking windows and sporadic gunfire.

Nell shivered with fear and looked to the physician for reassurance. 'They . . . they want to hang us both, don't they Doctor Hawkins?'

The doctor looked back with a pained expression. 'I'm afraid so, Nell. And I just hope the mob didn't storm the jail. It sounds as though things have gotten out of hand and turned into a full-blown riot.'

Nell looked horrified and bit the back of her knuckles. 'W . . . will they come here, do you think?'

Doc Hawkins had poured a medicine glass full of a cherry-coloured liquid. He advanced towards her and held it out. 'No one will think to look here, so you'll be safe with me,' he said soothingly. 'Now I want you to drink this. It's a concoction of valerian of my own invention. It will help to steady your nerves.'

But as Nell raised the glass to her lips, the rear door burst open and Frank Wheeler rushed in. Nell started, spilling half the contents of her glass over Jeff s face, causing him to rally back to wakefulness.

Wheeler rushed past them, bizarrely oblivious to their presence. Instead he dropped to his knees by the window. 'Harrington's dead!' he announced over his shoulder. 'And Mallory's after me!'

He shattered the window with the barrel of his gun and fired twice in succession at some target outside in the shadows.

Doc Hawkins cried: 'For God's sake, stop! Don't shoot!'

But Wheeler ignored him. Instead he shouted, almost in desperation: 'It's over, Doc. It's Mallory or — '

He never finished the sentence because there was the crack of a gun and the back of his head exploded in a spray of blood and brains, and his body was propelled forward to rest half in and half out of the window.

Nell screamed, unable to comprehend what had happened. Then a moment later the door was carefully pushed open and Tom appeared, his twin Navy Colts in his hands. He took in the scene in front of him — Nell and Jeff holding each other's hands, the body of Frank Wheeler hanging out the window with his brains blown out — and Doc Hawkins standing with a smoking gun in his hand.

Doc Hawkins nodded. 'I got him for

you, Tom. He said he'd killed Chester Harrington.'

Tom nodded. 'He killed Harrington, all right.'

'Then I guess it's all over. I finished it for you.'

The noise of the mob at work outside, shooting, breaking down doors and windows, looting, was impossible to ignore.

'It looks like it, Doc,' said Tom. 'But things aren't always how they look, are they?'

Nell jumped to her feet. 'Nothing's ever clear around here, Tom. I'm just grateful that Doctor Hawkins thought of getting us to come over here to safety.'

The physician reached out a hand reassuringly. 'I told you it would be safe here, Nell.'

Tom cocked the hammer of one of his Colts. 'Like I said, Doc. Things aren't always as they seem. Now drop the gun!'

In an instant Hawkins had grabbed

Nell's wrist and pulled her to him, pressing the gun barrel to her temple with his other hand. He smiled. 'Why Tom, maybe you're a tad smarter than I imagined.' His face hardened. 'Now you drop your guns. Now!'

Tom uncocked the gun then let them both drop.

'Now put your hands behind your head and kick those guns over here.'

Again, Tom acquiesced.

'Let — Nell — go!' gasped Jeff, struggling to sit up.

'No Jeff,' Nell whispered, her eyes wide like a frightened rabbit. 'Just do whatever he says.'

Doc Hawkins laughed. 'The voice of reason, gentlemen.' He nodded his head to indicate the noise of the mob outside. 'Unlike what is happening out there. Possibly there'll be a death or two, a few wounds that they'll want the good town doctor to deal with in the morning.'

'It's all been a game to you, hasn't it Doc?'

The physician pursed his lips. 'Yes and no. I've done a good job in this town and hereabouts. Medicine and surgery are important to me. I even enjoy delivering nesters' babies in the middle of the night. But a doctor's fees aren't exactly going to make me rich.'

Tom nodded. 'Whereas the Diamond T is.'

Hawkins laughed. 'The Diamond T? That moth-eaten ranch!'

'But you've been conniving to get it for a long time, haven't you Doc?'

A nod of the head. 'True. I rather enjoyed recruiting my troops, my minions, then setting them to work for me.'

'That's what I figured,' said Tom. 'And as a doctor you were in a prime position to diagnose folk's weaknesses — right?'

Doc Hawkins laughed. 'Right again, Tom. Take Chester Harrington and his sciatica. It was child's play to get him addicted to a mixture of laudanum and valerian. Without his fix he lived in constant agony. My drugs made him — amenable.' Then as if remembering that he had Nell in a necklock with his gun pressed against her temple, he eased off the pressure of the gun. 'In fact, you were about to sample the delight of my little concoction, Nell. Before that imbecile Frank Wheeler so rudely interrupted us.' He laughed again. 'He deserved to die for that alone.'

'And how did you manage to bend Frank Wheeler to your will?'

Hawkins shrugged as if the matter had been simplicity itself. 'Greed, pure greed. The man was a ruffian with no scruples. By using him I could get everyone to think that Sam Wheeler was behind things. Frank of course was itching to get the ranch and was not averse to killing his uncle. And of course he hated you, Tom. Ever since you humiliated him in front of half the town. That's why he was happy to set your girlfriend's place on fire and try to smoke you out.'

'And he killed Sheriff Milburn and then Zach Fargo. And I guess he took care of Rusty as well.'

This brought an almost maniacal laugh to the lips of the town doctor. 'The sheriff? Oh yes, he and Jarvis shot him, but I finished him off after you so kindly delivered him to me. As for Zach Fargo and Rusty, well don't you realize? That was pure artistry — that was me again.'

For a moment Tom lost his calm countenance. Anger and hatred flashed across his face and he had to steel himself from hurling across the room. But he realized that any such attempt would almost certainly result in Nell's death and probably that of Jeff and himself before he even reached the doctor. Instead, he tried to collect himself as his mind went over the moment he discovered the bloodbath in the jail. It all flashed before him and he recollected Rusty saying to get the doctor. He had assumed it was because he wanted help, not that he was telling him the name of his murderer, the man who had stabbed him.

'I was amazed that he survived that long, actually,' went on Hawkins. 'I stabbed him straight through the heart. Ninety-nine men out of a hundred would have died instantly.'

Noise seemed to be coming from all over the town and, somewhat incongruously the pianist at the Four Kings had started to play. Tom nodded his head in its direction.

'So what hold did you have over Tyler Kent?'

Hawkins grinned. 'A little blackmail over his — indiscretions! He is, for want of a better word, a lecher, you see. And a murderer.'

'Care to elaborate?' Tom asked.

'Betsy-May Elmore. The girl he raped and strangled.'

Nell immediately stiffened, but said nothing. Jeff, on the other hand, understood only too clearly. 'The scum! He made out that my paw did it! And that means that you — '

Hawkins laughed again. 'That I knew about it. Of course I did. And it was a good way of getting rid of Jake Trent.'

Tom clicked his tongue. 'And you tried to get me to think that he might have been covering up for Jeff. That trick with the red hair. And your other trick was getting your men to rough me up?'

'Now that did work. You thought I was your friend,' Hawkins volunteered.

'And then you got them to murder Digger Brown?'

Hawkins shrugged. 'He was a damned drunken fool. He was bound to tell people about his find before I was ready. And of course, he wasn't the first — '

Tom interrupted: 'Not the first prospector. I know. I got the padre to let me see the church register of all the recent burials in the Pasco Springs cemetery. I guessed that you'd bumped off a few more prospectors.'

The physician laughed. 'Four to be precise. Otherwise they'd have spread the news about the copper!' And at mention of the word his eyes glistened, much as they had done on the occasion that he'd given Lucinda some electro-therapy with one of his batteries.

'And that's why you wanted the Diamond T,' Tom mused. 'So that you could have complete access to the mountains without risking a rush.'

'Exactly, and once I've dealt with you three I can put my plan into place and start on my way to being the richest man in the south-west.'

Jeff had pushed himself up to a sitting position and looked as if he was contemplating making a do-or-die rush. But Hawkins tightened his grip on Nell's neck and pushed the gun firmly against the side of her head.

'Don't even think about it,' he warned. 'I'd as soon make this easy for you all, and I'd rather not start with a woman. Especially not when I've just saved her from one particularly unpleasant way to die. For now!'

* * *

The leaderless mob had soon disintegrated into various rampaging groups. Once things had gravitated away from the sheriff's office Jack told Elmer Ludvigsen to get Wes Lake out of harm's way, while he, Clem and Leroy tried to track down Tom.

'Whatever we do, we gotta prevent Frank Wheeler from leaving town,' Jack said to Clem and Leroy, as they warily made their way down the street.

'Then we better round up every horse in sight,' suggested Leroy.

And as they separated to go horse gathering Jack silently prayed that Tom was still alive.

* * *

'You'll never get away with this, Doc,' Tom said.

Doc Hawkins smirked. 'On the contrary, Tom. I already have.'

'Maybe you're too confident, Doc. Maybe you've just put your neck in the noose.' He smiled. 'In fact, I'm betting that you're gonna hang.'

Hawkins shook his head pityingly. 'You and your gambling, Tom. It'll be the death of you one day.'

But the smile had not faded from Tom's face. 'No, I mean it, Doc. Thanks for the confession.'

The town doctor stiffened as from behind him there was the unmistakable ratchet noise and click of a hammer being drawn back. It was followed by Lucinda's quavering voice: 'Drop that gun now, Doc. I've already put one filthy animal down tonight and I'm in no mood to pussyfoot around with another.'

For a moment they all stood motionless. Then the unexpected happened. The front door was thrown open and Elmer Ludvigsen came stumbling in with Wes Lake.

'Hey Doc? Where are you? I've got Wes and he's badly wounded and losing bl — '

It was the momentary distraction that Hawkins needed. He threw Nell forward towards Jeff and Tom, then elbowed Lucinda in the stomach. He turned, grabbed her by the back of the neck and hurled her into the room.

Her gun went off, almost simultaneously with his, as he shot Wes Lake between the eyes and put a bullet in Elmer Ludvigsen's arm. He barged Elmer out of the way and with a couple of bounds he was out the door.

Lucinda managed to save herself from falling flat on her face. As she regained her balance she saw Tom pitch forward onto the floor with blood streaming down his face.

* * *

Tom's eyes flickered open and he slowly came back to consciousness, to see four pairs of worried eyes looking down at him. Nell and Jeff had their arms about each other. Elmer Ludvigsen, as pale as alabaster with a wounded arm — and Lucinda, looking worried beyond belief.

'Tom — I . . . I thought I'd killed

you,' she gasped.

Tom put a hand to the side of his head, which felt as if it had been hit with a red-hot poker, and found it to be wet and sticky with blood.

'Lie still,' said Lucinda. 'We need to tend to that wound.'

But Tom was on his feet, albeit unsteadily, in a moment. 'The hell I do! I've got to get that murdering dog.'

'Yes and I'm coming with you!' said Elmer.

But a glance at him showed otherwise. Tom shook his head as he gathered a Navy Colt from the floor. 'Look after Elmer, Lucinda. And if any of the deputies come in, tell them I've gone after Hawkins.'

Bursting out of the door into the moonlit street, Tom was immediately struck by the mayhem that had been caused. Broken windows, a couple of fires from discarded kerosene lamps, and a lot of noise from the Four Kings. The sound of galloping hoofs from the end of the street sent him sprinting towards the livery, where he found Leroy slowly pushing himself to his feet. His sombrero lay in the dust and he had a nasty gash across his forehead. 'That cur clubbed me, Tom,' he said groggily.

'Doc Hawkins?'

'Th . . . think so,' replied the lanky cowboy.

Tomb dashed into the livery and swiftly saddled the roan. A few moments later when he rode it out, Leroy was hanging onto a post for dear life, having just vomited.

'I'm going after him, Leroy,' Tom shouted. 'When you're feeling able, go get Jack and tell him which direction I've gone.'

And with that he urged the roan into a gallop in pursuit of the errant physician. It was not an easy ride by moonlight, but the roan was as sure-footed a piece of horseflesh as he had ever ridden. It seemed to know what was expected of it. Within a few minutes he had started to catch up on the fleeing doctor.

Upon realizing that someone was in hot pursuit, Hawkins turned in his saddle and cursed when he recognized Tom. He fired twice, the first bullet whistling past Tom's left cheek. The second bullet hammered into his left shoulder, just as he was about to return fire, knocking the gun from his hand.

Somehow Tom managed to stay in the saddle, more motivated now by hate and anger than by logic. For he was weaponless, while the man he wanted to overhaul still had his gun. But Tom was determined to either take him or die. And as the roan thundered after the doctor on the cow pony, Tom reached for the lariat attached to his pommel.

Weak from blood loss he managed to loose the rope and one-handedly build a loop. A few jabs with his heels and the roan closed the gap. He drew the rope back, then tossed the hoolihan, watching it sail out towards its target. Fifteen, twenty, twenty-five feet; in the moonlight it seemed to travel in slow motion, until it dropped down towards the doctor on his galloping cow pony. And in that instant the doctor turned and fired. Tom felt a stab of blinding pain, then utter blackness.

* * *

When Tom came to, he found Jack Fisher kneeling beside him, relief written across his face. 'I thought you'd bought it, Tom.'

Tom struggled to a sitting position, aware that he hurt just about everywhere, presumably from his fall. Then he realized that in addition to his head and shoulder wounds, he had sustained another graze about an inch above his first temple wound.

'Your luck held out, Tom,' Jack said. 'Any closer and you would've been swapping that star for a harp.'

Only then did Tom see the group of deputies a little further off standing nearby the roan. The rope was still attached to the pommel of his Texas rig, leading all the way to a dark shape on the ground by the feet of the standing deputies. With Jack's help he hobbled over and saw that the shape was indeed that of a man. The open eyes illuminated by moonlight belonged to Doc Hawkins. The noose had been pulled tight about the neck, while the head lay at an impossible angle to the torso.

'Well what do you know,' Tom mused. He looked down at the dead man, feeling no pity for the manner of his death. 'Looks like you were destined to die by the rope, you sick bastard!'

⋆ ⋆ ⋆

Over the next week Pasco Springs slowly returned to normality. Or as close to normality as it could ever hope to achieve. A cloud of shame hung over it, and every man who had allowed himself to be sucked into the mob reacted to his own personal shame. Some drank themselves to oblivion, others went about their business as usual then went home at night and kicked their dog. But the majority aimed to make amends. And like a wounded prophet, Elmer Ludvigsen showed them the way. Although grieving for his friend Wes Lake, he was as busy as a bee in the first flush of summer. By example he got a community spirit rolling. Neighbour helped neighbour, friend helped friend, and even bitter rivals helped one another.

Tom Mallory, a bandage about his head, watched and approved of the actions of a mayor in the making. And mercifully, as his wound healed, so he was able to take time to sort out affairs. He prepared a detailed report for the impending arrival of the circuit judge.

When Judge Tulloch finally came, the cases against Nell and Jeff Trent were dropped with little ado. At the inquest the web of deceit and skulduggery that had been spun by the town doctor and his henchmen was uncovered and, though the perpetrators were all dead, the judge as good as passed a posthumous sentence upon them all.

'And to the Trent family,' he announced, 'I can only offer my deepest sorrow over the unlawful killing of Mr Jake Trent by persons unknown. I declare that he was clearly innocent of any crime.'

Jeff Trent, nearly recovered from his wound, sat comforting Nell. Gone was the look of hatred and contempt, replaced now by the obvious feelings that he held for the beautiful woman beside him.

And with the criminal cases taken care of, Judge Tulloch gave his considered opinions on the probity issues relating to Rusty Reardon and Curly O'Toole. Further, the situation regarding the debt owed by the Diamond T to the bank was taken care of after testimony from the new Pasco Springs bank manager, Joe Watkins, who was able to substantiate Nell Trent's statement that the debt was no more than twelve hundred dollars.

Later, over dinner at the Diamond T, Tom and Lucinda sat and enjoyed the meal that Nell set before them. It was an alcohol-free occasion, since Jeff announced that he had taken the pledge. 'I promised Nell,' he told them.

'What are you planning to do about Digger Brown's copper strike, Tom?' Nell asked.

Tom shook his head. 'Absolutely nothing, Nell. I talked it over with Judge Tulloch and unofficially we agreed to leave out all mention of it. I think it's better if it just stays in the mountains where it belongs. There's been too much blood spilt over the red metal already.'

'So you're set on being a rancher after all?' Jeff asked.

Tom winked at Lucinda, then turned to the younger man. 'Before I answer that Jeff, tell me one thing — what are your intentions towards Nell?'

Jeff Trent's cheeks suffused with red, only matched by Nell's blush. 'I . . . I think I'm going to ask her — to marry me.'

Nell let out a small shriek, then flung her arms about his neck.

'In that case,' said Tom, squeezing Lucinda's hand, 'I'm not going to be a rancher after all. You are!'

Both Nell and Jeff stared uncomprehendingly.

'It's a wedding gift,' Lucinda explained, with a twinkle in her eyes. 'Before we came out here this evening we thought we'd cut cards about the future.'

Tom slid his arm around her shoulders and kissed her cheek. 'But we didn't need to. We decided that Lady Luck had already given us all we need.'

'Each other,' whispered Lucinda.

THE END